DANGEROUS INFURMATION

A WHISKERS AND WORDS MYSTERY
BOOK TEN

ERYN SCOTT

KRISTOPHERSON
PRESS

Can't they have a *meowment* of peace?

A string of robberies has Button and its neighboring cities on edge. Lou, whose bookstore was the first business targeted, is eager to figure out how to stop the thieves. Before she can, Lou's neighboring business owner is killed during a robbery gone wrong.

Desperate to seek justice for her friend, Lou can't help but get involved. But things become more complicated when the thieves begin secretly returning the items they stole from her. The books become clues that just might help Lou figure out who's behind the crimes.

It's a race against time as new businesses are hit every few days. Can Lou put a stop to it before anyone else is robbed? Or worse, murdered?

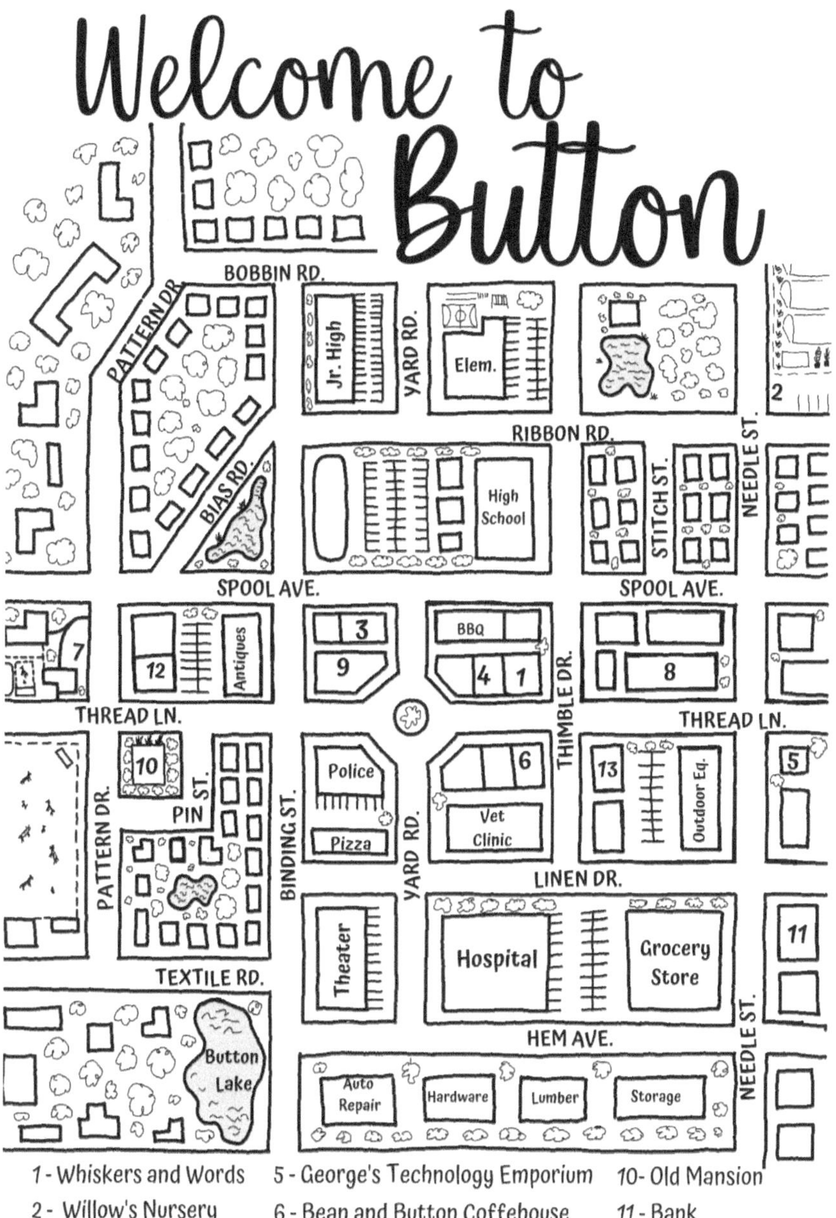

1 - Whiskers and Words
2 - Willow's Nursery
3 - Button Bistro
4 - Scoop O' Button
5 - George's Technology Emporium
6 - Bean and Button Coffeehouse
7 - Willow and Easton's houses
8 - Material Girls
9 - The Upholstered Button
10 - Old Mansion
11 - Bank
12 - Pet Store
13 - Bakery

CHAPTER 1

Louisa Henry's sneakers scuffed along the concrete sidewalk in front of her bookstore as she came to a stop after her morning run. She swiped at the sweat gathering on her forehead and took a deep breath to regulate her heartbeat.

Once her pulse slowed, she stepped up to the bookshop's front door, readying her key. The deep purple leaves and bright pink flowers of the matching smoke bushes sitting on either side of the front door made her grin.

Not only were they beautiful, they were also on loan from Willow's nursery. They reminded Lou of her best friend's support. Though the bushes were technically for sale, and Lou had sold quite a few of Willow's plants by featuring them in front of her bookshop, the upgrade to the appearance of Lou's storefront made her feel like she always came out ahead with their arrangement.

If the vibrant plants at the entrance hadn't already put a smile on her face, the small herd of cats that raced over to the door would have definitely done the job. Whiskers and Words wasn't just a bookshop, it was also a rescue cat sanctuary—a safe place for cats to live while they waited to find their forever homes. Each of the cats inside was available for adoption.

Well … except for one. Sapphire, the all-white deaf cat with the **Not for adoption** collar, was Lou's cat, and he was here to stay.

Sapphire was also less inclined to give up his sunny spot in the front window to say hello to her. Lou walked over to him, planting a kiss on his head. She missed him during the evenings when she went home to her new house. The few times she'd tried bringing him with her when she went home at night, he'd wandered around the house, crying out for the other cats.

Living off the premises was still a new sensation for Lou. She had gotten used to the small apartment above the bookshop. But she couldn't beat the happiness she felt at getting to live with Noah and next to their best friends, Willow and Easton, to boot.

"Good morning, everyone." After greeting Sapphire, Lou beamed down at the fosters whom she'd given punny literary names—all except Meatball, who'd been discovered in an alley in the city with a ball of meat clamped between her teeth. Lou hadn't had the heart to change the sleek tortoiseshell's name. The rest of them, however, had been renamed things like Anne Mice, Catnip Everdeen, Charles Lickens, Mr. Clawrcy, and Jane Pawsten. The fosters rubbed up against her legs, meowing the whole time. Anne Mice, always the most affectionate, rose onto her back legs, asking to be picked up.

"Let me take a shower first, Annie Girl, or I'm just going to get you all sweaty," Lou explained to the cat, who dropped back down on all fours. "This summer's going to be a scorcher if it's already this hot and it's only May."

After feeding them and cleaning their litter boxes, something she did every morning and evening, Lou jogged upstairs to her old apartment. Even though it was mostly empty now, she appreciated having a place to shower at work, especially when she opted to go on a run before opening the store. And lately, her runs had become quite lengthy.

She'd been checking on the houses of two local women while they were out of the country on vacation. Beverly, a retired bus driver with a penchant for gardening, and Evelyn, the retired high school librarian, lived on opposite sides of town. So, checking on their houses on foot meant that Lou got in a good, long run.

Patting her phone, she slipped it out of the pocket of her running pants. Exercise hadn't been the only positive outcome from house-sitting for the two retired friends. It was during her time watering their plants and getting their mail that she'd first sighted the large, orange cat she'd named Lemewl Gullipurr—instead of Lemuel Gulliver— after his epic travels. Sighting an outdoor cat wasn't much of an oddity in the small town of Button, Washington. But the fact that she'd seen the orange cat on completely opposite ends of the town, and only days apart, had piqued her interest.

Since then, she'd found him in increasingly surprising locations, doing increasingly interesting things. Seeing what the curious feline was doing or where he popped up next became a favorite pastime. Lou had even begun a blog on the bookstore's website entitled *Gullipurr's Travels*, which chronicled his adventures around Button, including pictures when she could snap them.

That morning, she'd caught an especially cute photograph of him stalking a field mouse in the meadow next to Evelyn's home. She chuckled to herself as she realized she could caption it: *Lemewl Gullipurr meets his first Lilliputian.*

She'd been able to make multiple references to the classic novel already. A snapshot of Gullipurr hiding from a Great Dane made for the perfect caption: *Gullipurr isn't sure about the giant Brobdingnagians.* And even a candid shot of him standing on a rock surrounded by water on the edge of Button Lake that she captioned *Gullipurr's ship, stranded after a pirate attack.*

The locals loved it, sending in their own pictures when they had a Gullipurr sighting, and even asking Lou to order in more copies of the classic novel for them.

After a quick shower, Lou raced downstairs and began uploading the pictures of the orange cat, writing out a little description of the date, time, and weather when the photo had been taken. Then, glancing over at the box sitting open on the table next to her checkout counter, Lou added one more line:

The special illustrated editions of *Gulliver's Travels* have arrived! If you were hoping for a copy, come in soon because I have a feeling these are going to go *Swift*-ly.

She grinned at her use of the author's last name and hit

publish on the newest blog. Lou was just about to start the rest of her opening chores when she was startled by a knock on the bookshop's front door.

Two men stood outside. She'd only barely noticed the harried looks on their faces when her attention was swept away by what one of them held in his arms.

A kitten. White. Tiny. Dirty. Obviously sick.

It clung to the man's shirt. Lou's heart jumped, remembering when Sapphire had been that size. She raced over to the door, unlocking it and ushering the men inside.

"Thank goodness," one of them said. "We found this little guy in our friend's barn and didn't know where else to take him. We saw on your signage out front that you take in fosters."

Lou nodded, though her focus was locked on the cat. "Yes, that's correct."

Through the fog of her concern, Lou clocked that they hadn't closed the door behind them. While none of her current fosters were bent on getting outside, she'd had escape artists before, and she didn't like to tempt any curious felines. She stepped back toward the checkout counter, thinking the men weren't closing the door because they didn't have enough room.

They stepped forward but still didn't close the door. Lou was about to ask them to when the one with the kitten held it forward. The tiny thing sneezed. Its eyes were almost crusted shut, and its small chest heaved in and out with rattling breaths.

Lou's heart clenched tight at the sight, scooping the sick kitten into her arms.

The moment the cat was out of the man's possession, his companion surged forward, grabbing the box of brand new, special edition *Gulliver's Travels* from the table next to Lou.

Before she could blink, the men sprinted out the open front door, taking the box of books with them.

Anger and confusion warred in Lou for the moments it took her to figure out what had just happened. Of course, they'd been here for nefarious reasons. Noah's veterinary clinic was on the next block over. If they'd truly been seeking help, they would've taken the poor creature there instead. Her worry for the kitten had clouded her judgment.

Balancing the kitten, she closed the front door before looking down at the pitiful thing. "You probably won't believe it after watching me fall for that, but I used to live in New York City."

The kitten sneezed, though it sounded more like a scoff.

LOU TEXTED Noah before she contacted law enforcement, knowing the kitten's health was the priority. But he'd been in the middle of an exam, so the police had beaten him to the bookshop.

Detective Easton West took down the information Lou remembered about the thieves—which was embarrassingly sparse, especially for someone who prided herself on possessing a detail-oriented mind.

"I'm sorry. I was so focused on the state of the kitten that I barely noticed the men. Obviously." She snorted, gesturing to the empty table where the box of books they'd run off with used to reside.

Luckily, Easton wasn't only her neighbor and landlord. He'd also become one of her close friends—and was rather in love with her best friend, Willow.

He placed a hand on her shoulder. "Don't beat yourself up, Lou. The thieves likely brought the kitten for that very reason—to distract you. We'll do our best to catch them."

What he didn't say was that it was unlikely they would be able to find them or her books. Especially with how little she'd been able to give him about their appearances.

There went a couple hundred dollars, blown on special illustrated hardbacks.

Lou huffed out a frustrated sigh. The only silver lining was that the kitten would be okay. Lou's ego would likely take longer to heal than the kitten would.

"She's got an upper respiratory infection," Noah explained when he showed up a few minutes later. His brawny arm curled around the feline, making it appear even more diminutive than it had in Lou's embrace. "She looks terrible, but this'll all clear up with some antibiotics."

"She?" Lou's tone lilted up as she tilted her head, considering the kitten.

Noah nodded. "I suspect a bath will also reveal her to be a near miniature of Sapphire."

She had gorgeous blue eyes, the same feature on Lou's own cat that had been so striking, it led to his name. Lou glanced over at her cat. "It was what drew me to her at first —how much she looks like he did as a kitten. But I think she's half the size that he ever was."

"She is tiny," Noah said, holding her up so he could see her better. "I can take her with me, if you don't mind me grabbing a crate from the back." Noah handed the kitten over to Lou, who shook her head to show that she didn't mind at all.

She stared into the kitten's jewel-toned blue eyes. Snapping her fingers in an arc around the kitten's head, she confirmed that it could hear just fine, as opposed to Sapphire, who was deaf.

"You sure are tiny," Lou told the animal. She was reminded of her blog post that morning. "I feel like you might be a Lilliputian. Or a *Lillipurrtian*." She gasped happily, causing the kitten to flinch away at the noise. "Sorry. I got excited."

"About?" Noah asked, approaching with a crate.

"Calling her Lillipurrtian since she's so small."

Noah chuckled. "Lilli for short?"

"Perfect." Lou placed her inside the open crate. She planted a kiss on Noah's cheek and thanked him for his help.

Once Lou finally opened that morning, her first customer inquired about the *Gulliver's Travels* special editions, and she had to break the bad news right away.

That continued over the next few days, and by Sunday, Lou suspected everyone in town had either heard what happened or had seen her announcement on the website, letting everyone know she was waiting on a replacement order to show up. At least the questions had stopped. Even better, Noah texted to let her know that the kitten, who'd been staying at the clinic so he could monitor her progress, was finally looking well enough—and flea-free enough—to come home with them that evening.

They'd decided that she was just too small to have loose in the bookstore. There were too many opportunities for her to slip outside unnoticed or show up underfoot. They would keep her at their house for the time being. She sent off a text to Noah in response.

> Maybe we should bring Sapphy home too, so Lilli has some company.

That sounds like a great idea.

> I've got the chamber of commerce meeting in a few, so I'll text you when I'm done.

Lou had run to work again, having done her Beverly and Evelyn rounds early that morning.

I'll be ready. Enjoy the meeting!

> Thanks!

She and Heather, the woman who owned the clothing boutique behind Lou's bookstore, usually attended the meetings each month, but this one was extra important because a financial expert from Seattle was coming to do a presentation on money management for small businesses.

Speaking of Heather, Lou checked the time and texted the woman. They'd taken to chatting in the alley between their buildings in the mornings and had planned to walk over to the meeting together.

Almost ready?

Heather responded immediately.

Actually, I'm just finishing up some ordering that I've been putting off and I'm so close that I'm afraid, if I stop now, I'll never get it done. Do you think it'll be awful if we show up a little late?

It was five minutes to the start of the meeting, but Lou shook her head as she wrote back.

Not at all. You know how much chatting and cookie eating goes on in the beginning. They're not going to start that presentation until they go through the minutes from the last meeting. I'd say if we arrive within the first hour, we're fine.

Lou couldn't help but grin at the thought. She loved the other Button business owners, but getting them to sit down and be quiet felt akin to herding kittens. Add in some of Lindsey's famous sugar cookies, as she always brought for the meetings, and they were a distractible lot.

Great. I'll meet you on Thread Lane in thirty, then.

Lou gave Heather's message a thumbs-up, and then she picked up her feather duster and got to work on her shelves. They could always use a dusting.

As was also always the case, a small group of wide-eyed felines followed her as she swooped the stick with feathers on it through the air. The group usually dissipated the moment they began sneezing from the dust, but their predatory instincts and feline curiosity never failed to make Lou smile for the first minute until the novelty wore off and they wandered away.

It was just after Lou's feline audience had dissolved, and they'd gone back to lounging about in the evening sunbeams streaming through the windows, that a loud *bang* caused Lou to jump. Charles Lickens and Mr. Clawrcy galloped out of the back office.

"What did you boys knock over?" Lou asked, waving her feather duster at them in a scolding way.

But when she walked into the back room, she couldn't find anything that could've fallen to create such a racket. Confused, Lou went back to her dusting, waiting until she'd given Heather a full half hour to finish her ordering. Locking up, Lou rounded the building and stood on the sidewalk in between their two businesses on Thread Lane, waiting.

It wasn't until she'd been standing there for five minutes that Lou decided to poke her head into the clothing boutique to see if Heather was ready.

That was when the flashing lights of police cars parked in front of the boutique caught Lou's attention. Heart picking up, along with her pace, Lou jogged over to where Easton stood next to the boutique's front door.

Lou didn't even get a word out before Easton's hand was on her shoulder again in consolation, just like the other day after her bookshop had been robbed. This time, however, there was a sadness and anger in Easton's eyes that hadn't been present when it had just been books Lou had lost.

"Someone robbed Heather. I don't think they expected her to be here or to be armed, but they turned the gun against her." Easton's throat bobbed in a hard swallow. "She was dead by the time we arrived."

CHAPTER 2

Spool Avenue spun around Lou. While she was no stranger to death, rarely did it hit this close to home for the bookshop owner. Heather was a friend. They saw one another in the alley between their buildings all the time, chatting about what was new in their lives. Heather had recently gotten back from a solo trip to Italy. Lou had seen her vacation pictures. Half of Lou's wardrobe had been purchased from Heather's store.

And now she was gone.

Lou made sure she kept her back to the boutique. She didn't want to see anything. She wanted to remember Heather how she'd been in life.

"It just happened?" Lou's voice was hoarse.

"About fifteen minutes ago," Easton confirmed. "Dusty called, saying he was sure he heard a gunshot, but it's his busy time, and he couldn't take the time to investigate."

Lou understood why the owner of the barbecue restaurant next door wouldn't be able to sneak away during the dinner rush. It was then that Lou realized she'd heard the shot as well. The loud noise she'd thought was simply the cats messing around in the office had, in fact, come from Heather's boutique.

Tears stung at Lou's eyes. "She was just finishing up ordering. I—"

But Lou didn't get the chance to finish that statement. A familiar voice interrupted her.

"What happened? Lou, are you okay?"

Willow's voice felt like a hug, one just as tight and grounding as the physical hugs she was famous for giving. Lou glanced up as her best friend jogged across the street, her tall frame tense with worry. Her brown hair was piled on top of her head in a bun, and Lou could see at least one twig caught in the mess.

"I saw the flashing lights from the nursery." Willow hooked a thumb behind her, as if her best friend and significant other might've forgotten where her business was located.

"Heather was robbed," Lou whispered. "They—they shot her."

Willow's hand rose to her mouth. "Was it the same guys who stole books from you the other day?"

Lou's gaze snapped up. "I hadn't even thought about that." Talk about losing her touch. Lou wasn't thinking about any of the connections or details she normally would have. She turned her attention to Easton. "Do you think they were the same?"

The detective exhaled. "Not that we can tell. Heather didn't have any security cameras, but it looks like they made away with some of her stock instead of money, just like with you. That could've been because they knew they needed to get out of here fast after the gun went off. The one thing we can tell is that the person who shot her was pretty tall." Easton held his hand to the top of Willow's head, then moved it up a few inches to the top of his. "Somewhere in this range, based on where the bullet entered and exited."

"The guys who robbed you didn't have a gun. Did they?" Willow asked, her skin taking on a sickly pallor as she considered the option.

"I didn't see one." Lou shivered at the reality that she could've met the same fate. Her stomach lurched in discomfort.

But Easton shook his head. "The gun is registered to Heather. She must've heard them break in and thought she could scare them away with the weapon. Instead, they used it against her."

"That sounds like a difficult thing to do, turning a gun against someone," Willow said. "Not like the guys who hit Lou and had to use a kitten for distraction."

Lou agreed with her friend. "What did they take from Heather?"

Easton glanced over his shoulder. "We haven't finished searching, but there's a rack close to the front door that's empty, save for one sweater. It's cashmere and worth almost two hundred dollars. So, depending on how many of them they were able to grab, they could've made off with a thousand or more in inventory. Given the time, I'm guessing they expected her to be gone for the evening."

"We were supposed to be," Lou whispered.

"Right." Willow snapped her fingers. "You two were going to the chamber of commerce meeting tonight."

"She needed a little extra time to finish ordering." Lou squeezed her eyes closed. "I told her it was fine, that we could be late for the meeting. People always linger over the cookies." She knew she was rambling, but she couldn't stop herself. Opening her eyes, she looked at her friends. "I should've insisted that we leave right away. I should've pushed her to go right then. If I had, she would still be alive."

"Oh, Lou. This isn't your fault. You can't blame yourself." Willow wrapped her in a tight hug, grasping her so fiercely that Lou couldn't breathe for a split second.

It was just what she needed. Still, as she stepped back from her friend's embrace, Lou ran her hands over her arms, though the temperature was still in the eighties—not cold at all.

"Did you run to work today?" Willow asked, having noticed the movement. "Do you need a ride home?"

"I did, but Noah's going to pick me up. I-I'll be fine." She tried to smile in reassurance, but she was sure it came out looking more like a grimace.

Waving to her friends, Lou walked back toward the bookshop. Out of the corner of her eye, she saw Easton wrap his long arms around Willow and plant a kiss on her forehead as she leaned into him. She couldn't wait to see Noah.

Pulling out her phone as she walked, she called him.

"That was quick. Did the speaker cancel? Were there no cookies?"

"Um, I didn't go. Would you come pick me up now? Heather..." Lou couldn't make herself say it at first. Inhaling for strength, she tried again. "Heather was shot during a robbery. She's gone, Noah." Her voice felt foreign, as if it wasn't hers.

He exhaled and swore under his breath. "Okay, I'm coming to get you now. I'll be there in a minute."

Instead of waiting outside for Noah, Lou let herself back inside the bookshop and paced. She curled her fingers in and out of fists, feeling helpless. What Easton said about Heather's lack of security cameras rang in her memory.

Heather might not have had surveillance set up, but Lou did.

The motion detector on the camera in the alley between their businesses hadn't gone off, which meant the thieves must've gone through the front door. But the reminder of how few details Lou had remembered about the robbers who'd stolen her books, and the occurrence of a second robbery next door, convinced Lou that her inside camera should probably be set to always record rather than recording only after business hours, as it was now.

She pulled up the software on her phone and fiddled with the timings like George, her techie friend and the town's personal *Geek Squad*, had shown her when the cameras had been installed. Lou had just changed the motion-sensor setting to always be on, when Noah entered the bookstore.

His brown eyes were shrouded in worry. He had brought a cat carrier, and he set it down on the table before continuing over to her, enveloping her in his strong embrace.

Lou exhaled and sank into him. "I forgot Lilli was coming home with us today," she murmured into his shirt, peeling back a little to get a better view of the tiny kitten in the crate on the table.

"Understandable," Noah responded with a slight uptick of his lips. "I didn't know how long you needed in here, and I didn't want to leave her in the car with how hot it is outside."

Lou appraised the kitten. "You look much better than last time I saw you, Lillipurrtian."

The kitten blinked her impossibly blue eyes at Lou from within the crate. Lou was happy to see that the respiratory infection seemed to be completely gone, and her fur was a crisp white now that she'd had a proper bath.

But when Lou turned to Noah, she found he was studying something other than the kitten. He was looking down at her phone, where the surveillance app was still open.

"Oh, I'm turning it on all the time, just in case. Apparently, I can't count on my brain to notice things, so the camera footage will be a nice backup if the thieves come back." She thunked the heel of her hand against her skull.

Noah gently took her hand in his, showing her she shouldn't beat herself up for that—metaphorically or literally. "That's going to be a lot of footage to go through," he said warily.

Lou opened her mouth, about to protest that it was worth it if it helped catch the people who killed Heather. But she didn't need to.

"If you add me to the account, I can help you go through it all," Noah added.

Feeling as though she might have literal hearts in her eyes as she gazed up at him, Lou balanced on her tiptoes to plant a kiss on his rough, bearded cheek. "Thank you." She input his number into the list to be notified when there was an alert. "I'll turn off the notifications during the day since we'll be drowning in them whenever the shop is open, and I'll put the cats upstairs during the evenings so they don't trip it. I just … if there's a way to catch these people, I have to try."

She didn't mention the guilt clouding her heart. If they were the same men who'd stolen from her the other day, this whole thing might've been avoided if she'd just paid attention to what they looked like. But Willow was right. It wasn't her fault. She knew from experience how easy it was to let the anger and sadness that followed losing a friend or a loved one manifest into feelings of guilt. One could drown in *what-ifs* and *if-I'd-onlys*. She'd done a lot of that when she'd first lost Ben, her late husband.

"Makes sense." Noah gave her a dimpled smile. "Ready to go home?"

The weight of the day settled over her at his mention of home. "More than ready." She sighed. "All four of us," she said, glancing from the kitten to Sapphire. "What do you say, Sapph? Want to help us get Lilli settled at home?" He blinked, which Lou took as a yes.

"Actually, there will be five of us. I was going to swing by and pick up Marigold on our way home, but I can drop you off first if you're not feeling up to going to Cass's." His brow furrowed. "Or, come to think of it, I could ask Cass if she wouldn't mind keeping Goldie for another night if you think that would be easier after everything you've gone through today."

The thought of not wanting Marigold around was

laughable. The eleven-year-old was an absolute bundle of joy, and Lou was under the impression that she made everything better.

"Oh, no." Lou cut the air with her palm. "After the day I've had, I *need* my Goldie fix. I don't mind coming with you either. I'd love to see Cassidy."

It was all true. It was also a testament to Noah and Cassidy's stellar communication skills how well things had gone over the past few months as Lou and Noah had moved in together, and Lou had become part of the parenting plan for Marigold. She'd already been so involved in the girl's life, watching her after school and having her help at the bookstore on weekends, that it hadn't been a huge adjustment for any of them.

Noah beamed, like that was just what he'd wanted to hear. "Great. I'll grab another crate for Sapph, if you want to get the kitten."

Once they had Sapphire in his own crate and the rest of the bookshop cats situated upstairs so they wouldn't set off the motion detectors, they drove toward Cassidy's cottage. Lou couldn't help but let her gaze linger on the boutique as they drove past, on the police cars still parked out front, and the reminder that her friend wasn't ever coming back. Tears finally streamed down Lou's face at the reality of it all.

CHAPTER 3

Lou's tears didn't last long. Her emotional breakdown was quickly upstaged by that of Lillipurrtian. The kitten wailed the entire drive to Cassidy's house. Lou cradled the carrier in her lap, whispering encouragements about how short the ride was and how they'd be home before she knew it. But the kitten only grew more distraught. Sapphire blinked at her from his crate in the back seat, unfazed.

The kitten's disdain for Noah's truck seemed to be limited to when it was in motion because her crying died down after he parked in front of his ex-wife's house. However, Lou was reticent to leave either cat in the cab, given the heat. Knowing they often chatted with Cassidy for a few minutes when they made these pickups, Lou decided the cats couldn't stay in the cab.

"You can't come all the way with us," Lou explained, holding Lilli's crate up to her face until she could see the kitten's bright blue eyes. "Cassidy's allergic to you. And while I don't think you'll set her off sneezing just being within a yard of her, we're not going to take any chances."

Marigold spent plenty of time around the cats at the bookshop. Cassidy couldn't live with a cat, but she wasn't so affected that a little cat hair on her daughter's clothing bothered her.

"This spot looks perfect." Lou placed the carrier in an area of Cassidy's front garden that was dappled with shade at the base of a small maple.

Noah set Sapphire's crate next to it. Lou wasn't sure if it was the outside air or the older cat that calmed her, but the kitten folded her legs under her, forming a little white loaf shape, and her blue eyes closed, content. That taken care of, Lou followed Noah up to Cassidy's porch.

"Hey," Cassidy greeted them as she stepped through the front door. "Is that the new little friend I've heard so much about?" She craned her neck to see the crate Lou had deposited in the garden.

"It is," Noah confirmed.

"Lillipurrtian," Lou added. "Lilli, for short."

"Marigold's very excited." Cassidy placed a hand on her chest and sighed at the cuteness. She must've just gotten back from showing a house because she wore one of her professional suits and her long blonde hair was curled in perfect waves—a quintessential Realtor, if Lou had ever seen one. "How'd the meeting go?" she asked Lou, checking her watch as if just realizing that Lou should technically still be there.

Lou gulped back the emotion that cropped up suddenly at the reminder of what had happened that evening. She'd tricked herself into momentarily forgetting as she'd tended to the crying kitten.

"Uh, I didn't go."

Lou glanced behind Cassidy into the house, making sure Marigold wasn't within earshot. The girl was well aware of the goings-on in town, but she'd also known Heather. If the closer-to-home nature of this death was hitting Lou harder than normal, she suspected it might do the same for Marigold.

Seeing they had some time before Marigold joined them, Lou said, "Heather's shop was robbed before we left for the meeting. She interrupted them and had a gun. They turned it on her and she's…" Lou couldn't make herself finish that statement, but Cassidy didn't need her to.

Cassidy took a gulp of air, raising a hand to her chest as her brown eyes swept between Lou and Noah. "That's awful." Moving her hand from her collarbone, Cassidy grabbed on to Lou. "You didn't find her, did you?"

Lou shook her head vehemently. "No. Thank goodness. Easton got the call. Dusty heard the gunshot from next door." She swallowed the sour taste in her mouth. "I guess I heard it, too, but I thought one of the cats had knocked something over in the office."

Small footsteps thundered through the house. A moment later, Marigold came racing out the front door with her schoolbag slung across her shoulder.

"What'd the cats do?" she asked, wrapping her arms around Lou's waist and squeezing tight.

Placing a hand on the mop of dark hair that matched her father's, Lou said, "I thought they were messing around in the office, but they were being good. Don't worry."

Marigold's brown irises shone as she moved her hug to Noah, greeting him as well. As she did, Cassidy stepped forward and surreptitiously fiddled with the zipper on Marigold's backpack. Slipping something out, she hurried it behind her back.

Lou may not have been able to brag about noticing details as of late, but that motion would've been difficult *not* to notice. "Was that—?" Lou cocked an eyebrow at Cassidy, having recognized the shape.

Cassidy huffed and produced a doll that was about a foot tall from behind her back. The doll wore what looked to be an outfit for a funeral, and her too-human eyes seemed to follow Lou no matter what direction she faced.

"Prudence!" Marigold shrieked out the doll's name. "How'd she get in my bag?" The girl danced with a shiver, proving she felt just as creeped out by the doll's appearance as the adults.

It was a running joke in the family, actually. Ever since Cassidy's mom had gifted the doll to Marigold last month, the adults had been trying to get the thing out of their respective houses. It had obviously started in Cassidy's home, but she'd planted it in Noah and Lou's house one day when she'd dropped Marigold off.

From then on, it had been a silent, silly war.

Cassidy's cheeks reddened as she addressed her daughter. "I snuck Prudence into your backpack as a joke, but now that I'm talking to Lou and your dad, I'm realizing that it might not be the day for pranks."

"Why?" Marigold squinted up at her mom, turning her questioning gaze on her father when no one answered.

Noah and Cassidy shared a meaningful look, one which

likely held an entire conversation about how to break the news to her. Noah gave a slight nod, apparently being the one chosen to speak. Lou watched the exchange in awe. The two might not have made it romantically, but they were an incredible team. And while it hadn't always been smooth, they worked hard to be on the same page when it came to their daughter.

"There was an accident today in town, petal," Noah said, kneeling so he was closer to his daughter's height. "Miss Heather, the one that owns the clothing boutique, she passed away." He placed a hand on his daughter's shoulder, squeezing tight as surprise flitted across her features.

"Oh, no." Marigold's gaze skipped up to Lou, making her heart ache. "Your neighbor."

Tears stung at Lou's eyes once more that day. Marigold dropped her bag and raced over to give Lou another tight hug. While she had her face buried in Lou's shirt, the adults gave one another sad looks, but they knew telling her had been the right thing to do. The children in the town of Button had their own rumor mill, one which was almost more efficient than that of the adults. She would've heard about it at school tomorrow, anyway.

"But we have Lilli and Sapphy coming home with us tonight to make everything better," Lou said as Marigold ended the hug.

That earned her a surprised grin. "I almost forgot! I can't wait to see how Sapphy reacts."

Lou didn't want the girl to get her hopes up too much. The older cat met most things with the same sleepy indifference these days, especially after living in Whiskers and Words with all the different foster cats that came and went.

If she had to predict what his reaction to Lilli would be, it was a blink of an eye and a swish of his tail—at most.

But she wasn't about to burst Marigold's bubble of excitement with practicality. "There's only one way to find out." Lou swept the girl toward the truck, leaving Noah and Cassidy to chat logistics about the next drop off.

She and Marigold stopped to grab the cat crates. By the time Lou had Sapphire and Marigold held on to Lilli's crate, Noah was walking in their direction with his daughter's schoolbag.

The trip home was a loud affair—thanks to Lilli— leaving everyone who *could* hear glad when Noah put the car in park. Normally, Lou would've commenced an intro- ductory period with a new cat, keeping the kitten in a room away from Sapphire for at least twenty-four hours so they could get used to one another's scent. But Sapphy had become an old hat at meeting new felines in the bookshop. Between that and Noah's assurances that Lilli was flea-free and healthy as could be, she figured the two would be candidates for a quicker introduction.

"She really is tiny," Lou observed as they let the white kitten out of the crate once they were settled inside. "I'm glad we brought her here. She definitely would've either gotten lost or trampled at the store."

Marigold followed the white ball of fluff around as she scampered curiously from one piece of furniture to the next, gently redirecting her attention any time she tried to claw something other than a scratching post. Sapphire watched the two of them, ears perked forward with interest.

"That's different," Lou mused as her cat walked over,

displaying more curiosity about Lilli than he had with another cat in a while.

"Good boy, Sapphy," Marigold cooed, holding out her hand to let him sniff before she pet him.

It was a tactic Lou's niece Maddy had taught Marigold when she'd visited during her spring break from college a few months ago. Maddy had always had an innate sense for how to interact with Sapphire in a way that worked with his deafness and made him comfortable.

Surprising Lou even more, Sapphire not only approached the kitten, but followed her as well. She felt Noah tense next to her, knowing that one reason for his sudden interest in the kitten could be anger, and he might be getting closer to give her a whap on the side of the head and a growl.

But neither of those things happened. Lilli raced over to Sapphy, rubbing up against the adult cat's legs. Sapphire leaned down, rubbing his face against her.

Marigold let out a long "Awwwww," while Lou placed a hand over her heart and Noah relaxed.

After that, Lilli went on exploring, with Sapphy following her, and Marigold tailing both cats. They did that for the better part of an hour as Lou and Noah made dinner. But by the time the family sat down to eat, the two white cats were curled up together in one of Sapphire's beds, purring contentedly, eyes shut to the world.

Lou breathed out a long sigh. "Well, at least one thing went well today," she said, checking her phone for alerts from the security system.

But it looked as if putting the cats upstairs had done the

job, and she didn't have a single notification. Noah checked his phone, too, placing a hand over Lou's and squeezing it.

"We'll figure out who did this," he whispered the moment Marigold finished her dinner and slid out of her chair to go snuggle with the cats.

Lou gave Noah a grateful glance, but worried he might not be able to make good on that promise.

CHAPTER 4

The next day, Lou drove to the bookshop. She didn't have the energy to run to work, let alone around town to check on Beverly's and Evelyn's homes. Driving would have to do.

She considered bringing Sapphire with her to the shop, but she opted to let him stay at home so he could keep Lilli comfortable while she acclimated to her new surroundings.

Speaking of acclimating, Lou wasn't doing a very good job of that herself. She hadn't considered that driving would mean she would have to park in the alley behind the bookshop—the same alley she shared with Heather's clothing boutique. The memory of Easton telling her the news yesterday felt like a vise steadily closing around her chest, making it hard to breathe.

With a shudder, Lou pushed past the feeling and unlocked the back door. The moment she opened the door hiding a staircase up to her old apartment, excited and hungry cats immediately ambushed her. After feeding them, cleaning their litter boxes, and showering them with attention, she made a sign for the front door warning customers they were being recorded. Once she'd posted that, Lou used the rest of her time before opening to finish the dusting she'd started last night. Dusting in any normal bookshop was critical, but it became even more important —and necessary—when there was an ever-changing number of foster cats living around the books.

So, she got to work, popping some music on the stereo system Noah had wired throughout the shop. Before long, the sounds of one of her favorite bands lulled her into a relaxed state, and the earlier tension released from her lungs.

But as she rounded the corner and headed down the biography-and-memoir aisle with the feather duster, that terrible feeling returned, tenfold.

There, sitting on the shelf, was a copy of *Gulliver's Travels*. One of the hardback special editions, with illustrations.

"Where did you come from?" Lou asked the book, as if it might answer back and solve the mystery.

Behind her, Charles Lickens meowed in response, causing her to giggle.

She was flipping through the pages, worry knotting her brow more with each cream-colored page that wafted by, when a knock sounded at the front door.

Poking her head out of the aisle, she spotted George standing outside. The first thing she noticed about her friend was the absence of her cat, Geralt. George often wore the clingy gray cat in a baby sling, walking about town with him strapped to her.

The second thing Lou noticed was George's outfit. In

her twenties, the young woman was usually clothed in fashions that were either approximately three sizes too big for her lithe body or looked—to Lou's forty-year-old gaze—like they might actually be lingerie. There didn't seem to be an in-between.

That day, George wore an outfit that fit solidly in the latter category. Her shorts were cut smaller than Lou's shortest running attire, and her tank top was more befitting of the beach than hanging around downtown.

Lou, however, was firmly aware of her prudish leanings and pushed all judgmental thoughts out of her mind as she jogged to the door to let her friend inside.

George rushed forward, pulling Lou into a tight hug. Her hair had been swept into a messy bun, and Lou got a face full of brown waves along with the embrace.

"I'm so sorry about Heather," George said.

Lou swallowed to buy herself a little time to get her emotions under control. She pulled back when some of George's hair tickled her nose.

"Sorry." George stepped back with a chuckle. "About the hair, too, not just Heather."

"No Geralt?" Lou asked, because that was easier than talking about her dead neighbor.

"Nah. He's a wimp and is much happier in the AC on hot days like today." She pulled her tight tank top about an inch away from her stomach as if to say even this small amount of fabric was too much for her in said heat. Her gaze zeroed in on the book in Lou's hands. "What's that?"

Blinking to regain her equilibrium, Lou said, "Oh. This is … uh, well … I'm actually not sure."

"It looks like *Gulliver's Travels*." George read from the

front cover, sounding worried that Lou might've forgotten how to read.

Lou chuckled. "I know *which* book it is. I'm just not sure how it got here."

"In a bookstore?" George didn't sound any less worried.

Lou laughed. "Because I ordered these for the store, but the entire box was stolen the other day before I could put them out."

That got George's attention. "Oh! Gotcha. And you're sure you didn't have any on the shelf beforehand?"

"Positive."

"So, how'd it get here, then?" George's lips twitched in confusion.

Lou shrugged. "Someone must have put it back. After what happened to Heather last night, I set the interior camera to record all the time, but that doesn't help me with this since I didn't make the change until after I closed." She tapped her fingers on the book's cover. "I wish I'd thought to turn it on right after those guys stole the books, but I honestly thought it was a one-off. That I'd never hear from them again."

"But between what happened to Heather and now this book showing up in your store, you're thinking they've come back?" George wrinkled her nose.

"I don't know what I think," Lou said, fatigue flattening her tone.

"Even if you *had* turned the interior camera on, that would be a lot of footage to look through." George puffed out her cheeks. "Speeding up the feed can only help so much."

Lou took the piece of information from her techie friend

to mean that she shouldn't beat herself up too badly for not having the foresight to do it sooner. "Well, at least now I can keep an eye out."

Glancing around the quiet bookshop, Lou noted that there was still ten minutes until the rest of the regulars would come filing through the door. She eyed her friend.

"So ... how's everything going?" Lou asked, taking advantage of it just being the two of them. "Dating life treating you well?"

It wasn't as if George was shy about talking about her love life in front of the other regulars, but Lou had a knowledge of the situation others didn't. A limited amount of it, anyway. That knowledge had come through a conversation Lou had with Wesley St. James, the man George was currently trying to get over.

It was during that conversation that Lou had encouraged Wesley to tell George if he had feelings for her. She wasn't sure if George dating other people meant Wesley hadn't yet told George how he felt, or if he had ... and she'd denied him. It was also possible that Lou had entirely misread the situation, and Wesley wasn't harboring romantic feelings for George, after all.

And while Lou didn't want to interfere—being a big believer that the two of them needed to figure out their relationship on their own—she liked to check in on her friend from time to time to see how she was doing.

The answer to Lou's question about dating was a resounding "Not great," based on the snort George let out in response.

"Most of the guys on the dating apps don't want anything serious. Who am I kidding? Most people *my age* aren't looking to 'settle down' yet." She used her fingers to put quotes around the phrase. "Yet another way I'm not like the people my age."

Despite her love of gaming and her much younger style choices, George had always fit in with the older crowd that lived in Button. George's upbringing by her grandparents and her early self-awareness of her goals made her a bit of an old soul.

"I wish I could meet someone like you and Willow did —the old-fashioned way." She pouted.

"None of the guys you've been on dates with have wanted a relationship?" Lou stashed the rogue book under the checkout counter.

George tilted her head to one side. "I guess that's not true. There have been a few. And don't get me wrong. They're nice, but there's no spark." She sighed.

Lou knew what a spark felt like. She'd had it with her late husband, Ben. And while she'd never expected to fall in love again, the spark between her and Noah had been undeniable from the moment they'd met.

She couldn't help but wonder if the spark George was waiting for was the kind she had with Wesley, and if convincing herself that Wesley was bad for her hadn't been some misguided way of rejecting him before he could reject her.

Before Lou could say something she would regret, meddling in other people's love lives, the front door opened, and two of Lou's other regulars strode inside.

Gloria and Cricket had taken to walking into town together most mornings. Cricket's house was on Gloria's way to the bookshop, and they both enjoyed the fresh air.

The walking seemed to be doing wonders for Gloria's back, which had become painful because of the stagnant lifestyle she had adopted after her son had been arrested the year prior.

Her back still bothered her sometimes and there was a slight bend to her spine that spoke of the pain she was in, but she had improved so much over the past few months.

Cricket and Gloria bustled forward, just as George had done, and wrapped Lou into tight hugs.

"I just can't believe Heather's gone," Cricket said. She plucked the shirt she wore. "I got this from her shop. And you all know how much I have to like something to buy it from a store."

The three other women nodded. Cricket was an accomplished seamstress, just like her best friend, Noah's mother. Most of her clothing was beautifully handmade, but Lou recently had noticed a few pieces from the boutique show up in her wardrobe.

Another one of Lou's regulars, Silas, walked in as they talked.

"I found the first dress I've liked in years at Heather's place," Gloria explained.

Silas plucked his signature bowler hat from atop his head. "She sold me this hat." His mouth tilted down as he studied the thing and then placed it back on his head. "Do you four think there's anything to the rumors that the robbery at Heather's store was connected to the robbers Lou had the other day?"

"Lou does," George answered for her, earning the young woman a scoff of surprise from Lou. "What? You do," George said in defense, pointing to the checkout counter. "You said yourself the robbers had been back to plant the book and to steal from Heather."

"What book?" Cricket placed a hand on her hip.

Lou reluctantly pulled the special edition out from where she'd stashed it. "I said I wasn't sure," Lou clarified. "But I did find one of the stolen books back on the shelf this morning. I turned on the interior camera to help me if they do come back, but I didn't do it until after what happened to Heather last night. Someone must have dropped it off during the time since these were stolen last Friday."

"You don't need a camera for that. I've got a list of suspicious characters who easily could've done that in the days following the theft." Silas tottered past Lou to the love seat where he always sat with Catnip Everdeen.

"What?" Lou asked, following him. "Who?"

"First and foremost, there was a man wearing two different shoes." Silas snorted. "They were pretty similar, but he couldn't pull one over on old Silas." He tapped his temple. "I saw the differences."

Lou, who'd grabbed a pen and paper to write down any descriptions, paused. She shot Silas an exasperated scowl. "Seriously?"

He eyed her in a *don't question me* kind of way before adding, "And then there were three women wearing the same color shirt within the span of an hour."

"What was the color?" Cricket asked flatly. "Blue?"

George, Gloria, and Lou all stifled laughs while Silas glared at Cricket.

"It was a very specific teal, I'll have you know." He lifted his chin. "And then there was the kid wearing lederhosen."

"Lederhosen?" Lou sputtered. "I didn't notice anyone wearing something like that."

Silas merely clicked his tongue as if that, right there, was proof of how she'd been robbed in the first place.

"And how'd you decide these people were up to no good?" Gloria asked in her rough voice.

Silas huffed. "Simple. None of them bought a single thing."

The confidence that had been building with Silas's words suddenly fell flat inside Lou. She fixed him with a dry look. "Um … I hate to break it to you, but if that's the only requirement to make the suspect list, all of you would be on it most days too."

A laugh burst out of George—one that Lou, Cricket, and Gloria echoed. Silas grumbled, focusing on Catnip as she jumped into his lap.

As good as the laughter felt, Lou couldn't help the feelings of unease that cropped up as she glanced down at the book in her hand. Little did she know that it wouldn't be the last of the stolen books to return to Whiskers and Words.

CHAPTER 5

Lou found the second copy of *Gulliver's Travels* a day later. A third showed up a couple days after that. And they continued like that for the next week—as did the thefts.

Button, Brine, and Silver Lake had all been hit at least once. There was never any consistency in the thieves' MO, according to Easton. Sometimes they struck during business hours. Sometimes after. Occasionally, the thieves wore costumes or used props to distract. Other times, they dressed normally, only obscuring their faces in situations where there were security cameras. One day, it would be two of them. The next time, there would be three, or even four.

The only consistent things linking the crimes were that they were all retail stores, the thieves would take multiples of the same high-ticket item—never cash, and the thieves were focusing on the three northern towns in Lakeside County.

This discovery led to the combined meeting of the

Button, Brine, and Silver Lake Chambers of Commerce. Lou, Willow, and George traveled to the meeting together that Sunday evening. Lou promised to fill Noah in since he stayed behind to pick up Marigold from fifth-grade camp. But judging from the crowded state of the meeting, most of the other local business owners were present.

"Of course we had to do this in Silver Lake," Willow muttered under her breath as they entered the community center of the larger city to the south.

Lou pressed her mouth shut, knowing not to push her friend about the real reason for her disdain of their sister city. While all Buttonites seemed to hold a similar negative opinion of Silver Lake—that they were stuck up and elitist—Willow's feelings were largely influenced by the fact that her sleazy ex-fiancé lived there now.

Lou scanned the space, but she didn't see James's tall frame or his current wife—the woman he'd been cheating on Willow with. George led them to a grouping of three seats near the back, and they filed into the row after her.

"Sorry, Lou," George said, leaning forward to see her around Willow. "You were telling us you found another book?"

Their conversation had been cut short when they'd arrived to find the parking lot of the Silver Lake community center absolutely bursting. It had taken all three of their keen gazes to find an open parking spot.

Nodding gravely, Lou said, "Just before I left. I haven't had a chance to check the security system yet. Noah said he'd watch through the last few days for me once Marigold inevitably crashes after getting home, but I'm guessing it's going to be like all the rest."

"Whoever dropped it off stays positioned in a way that you can't see their face?" Willow guessed, having heard Lou complain about the way the people who were leaving the books knew exactly how to keep their faces hidden from her camera.

Lou tapped the tip of her nose.

"How many is it now?" George asked, lowering her voice as the meeting started.

"Five," Lou said at the same time the man at the front of the room said the very same number.

She jolted in surprise, focusing on the young man who held the microphone.

Willow and George blinked at him, in just as much shock. Lou was about to ask how he'd heard their whispered conversation from all the way up there when he continued.

"Five businesses have been burglarized or robbed over the course of the last two weeks in Silver Lake, Button, and Brine." He straightened his shoulders as he looked out over the crowd, almost as if the group was larger than he'd expected and he needed to rally all his courage to continue. "Fellow business owners, my name is Austin Hunt. I own Silver Lake Books. The Silver Lake Chamber of Commerce has nominated me to speak to you today."

"I didn't know Rupert sold the bookstore in Silver Lake," Lou whispered to Willow.

It wasn't as if Rupert had liked her, at all—her first time in his shop, he'd just about kicked her out for comparing him to a man who'd died—so Lou hadn't expected him to tell her personally. Still, she at least thought she would've heard about this development through the local rumor mill.

Willow jerked her shoulders in a shrug, showing she hadn't heard anything either.

"Ugh. That hair is going to be the death of me," George whispered. She pinched the bridge of her nose and looked down.

Lou and Willow looked up to where Austin was still addressing the crowd, talking about the different businesses that the thieves had hit. He had dark, curly hair that flopped onto his forehead in a kind of debonair way. He had lips so full most women would kill to trade with him, and a warm smile full of big white teeth. Those teeth flashed as he went through a list of the items stolen from each business. And he looked to be just about George's age.

"I didn't realize you knew Austin." Lou leaned closer to whisper to George.

"But now that you mention it, the two of you would make an adorable couple," Willow added.

George's hand dropped, as did her jaw. She gaped at her friends, flicking a glance at Austin before scowling at them. "I wasn't talking about Austin," she hissed. "I was talking about *that* guy." George jerked her head to the left, to where Wesley St. James leaned against the wall closest to the exterior doors.

Wesley wore a cocky grin to match his devil-may-care stance, arms folded in front of himself. He'd also watched their whole interaction and held up two fingers in greeting as they finally looked over. His mouth twitched as Lou and Willow quickly waved back. George adjusted her messy bun farther to the left, as if her mass of hair might help hide her from the man.

"This guy, again?" Willow whispered. "I thought she

was over him." She directed that statement at Lou, but then repeated it for George. "I thought you were over him."

George sank lower in her seat and groaned.

Willow sucked a breath through her teeth. "Okaaay, so she's *not* over him."

A horrified gurgle was the only response from their friend.

They turned their attention back to Austin Hunt as he said, "And I don't know about you, but I don't feel like the local police are doing a thing about it."

Lou grabbed for Willow's hand as her friend stiffened beside her. It was hard for her to hear people speak poorly of the work Easton did. Willow nodded to Lou to signal that she was okay.

"They're just upset," Willow whispered. "You and I know that Easton and the others are working overtime and would like nothing more than to catch whoever's behind this. Our town's the only one that's experienced a death, after all."

Unaware of Willow's commentary, Austin went on. "Because of this, the Silver Lake Chamber of Commerce has pooled our resources and hired Private Investigator Wesley St. James to look into this matter for us, without the bureaucracy of local law enforcement." He held out his arm to welcome Wesley to the stage.

Wesley pushed off the wall and ambled up to the microphone with his usual swagger. He ran his fingers through his hair as he walked, tugging it into an effortless, side-swiped look that Lou was sure many men his age would've paid good money to achieve.

His lips crooked to one side, and he arched his dark

brows as he leaned down to speak into the microphone. "Hey, I'm Wesley. Thanks for trusting me with this. I'll do my best to figure out what's happening so we can prevent any further losses." His gaze washed over Lou, Willow, and finally, George. And then he exited, going back to stand where he'd been moments before.

Austin stepped back in front of the microphone. "I understand many people are pitching in to pay for this, and they'll want to know how the investigation is coming along. While we don't want to post anything that might give Wesley away to the thieves, if you have questions, feel free to contact me. I'll be in daily contact with Wesley about his progress." At that, Austin glanced over the crowd. "Button and Brine business owners, we're not going to turn away any monetary assistance you'd like to pledge to the cause. Brittany is handling the finances for this endeavor." He waved to a woman who stood in the front row. "If you'd like to donate, please see her at the end of the meeting." Austin cleared his throat. "Which is … now, I guess. As I mentioned before, if you'd please stick around at the end to see me regarding any tips or details you think might be helpful, that would be appreciated."

Lou blushed a little, having missed that part of Austin's speech due to all her whispering with Willow and George. She decided to make up for it by adding some money to the pot.

The surrounding crowd dispersed as people stood and broke off into smaller groups to chat, or they funneled up to the front to talk with Austin, Brittany, or any of the others Austin mentioned during his speech.

"I'm going to donate." Lou inclined her head toward Brittany.

Willow mumbled something about going to use the restroom.

George leaped forward, grabbing on to Lou's arm. "Please don't leave me alone." She shot a terrified glance over toward where Wesley had been standing, as if he were a wild animal and she worried for her life.

The space by the wall was empty. He was on the loose. George frantically scanned the room.

Lou almost laughed aloud at her reaction. "Fine, but that means you're coming up front with me." Linking her arm through George's, Lou pulled her toward the front of the room.

She wrote a check, making it out to the Silver Lake Chamber of Commerce. Once that was done, Lou saw a break in the line to chat with Austin. She sidled over, pulling George with her. His blue eyes were arresting as they held on to Lou, only moving to take in the sight of the pretty young woman next to her.

"Hello," Lou said, trying to break the tension. "I'm Louisa Henry. I own Whiskers and Words, the bookshop in Button." She held out her hand.

Austin shook it, his grip firm. "Right. Lou, it's great to finally meet you. Rupert mentioned there was a bookshop in Button." The way Austin coughed, shifting his weight in discomfort, told Lou that Rupert's opinion of her hadn't changed, and that he'd definitely shared it with Austin. But before Lou could say anything, Austin winked and added, "Don't worry, he didn't have much to say that was nice, or worth remembering."

She beamed her gratitude, then pulled at her bottom lip with her teeth. "Um … this might be a weird question, but have any of the other businesses reported having the stolen items returned?"

Austin studied her, confusion deepening the frown lines on his face.

Lou chirped out an awkward laugh. "Never mind. I just—"

"I hear you were the first business hit. They distracted you with a kitten?" Austin clicked his tongue in a tsk.

Cringing, Lou said, "Yeah. They did their research on me."

"In the name of research," Austin said, flashing his dazzling grin toward George, "may I ask who this is?"

"Oh, sorry. This is George Clark of George's Technology Emporium in Button." Lou swatted a hand toward her friend who finally seemed to abandon scanning the room for signs of Wesley.

Austin's mouth opened and closed a few times as he stood there, properly shocked. "*You're* the famous George everyone keeps bragging about?" He puffed out his cheeks, blinking for effect. "Wow. That's what I get for expecting a middle-aged man when everyone from Button told me about their tech genius named George. Serves me right, I suppose." He held out his hand.

George extracted her arm from Lou's to shake Austin's hand. Her cheeks blushed prettily at his compliment.

"She really is something. Isn't she?" a smooth voice said.

George stiffened next to Lou, and Lou found Wesley had swept in on George's other side. He'd slung his arm nonchalantly over her shoulders. George looked like she was simultaneously living a dream and a nightmare.

"You two know each other?" Austin's gaze flicked over Wesley's arm.

George gulped. "Uh, only—"

"Incredibly well," Wesley interrupted. "We've … collaborated on a few local cases. My PI skills and George's tech genius make us a rather unstoppable team. Wouldn't you agree, George?"

She glared at Wesley but schooled her expression, aware Austin was catching everything passing between them. "Yes, our working relationship has proven helpful in the past," she said through gritted teeth.

"Working relationship?" Austin coughed out a discomfited laugh. "That makes it sound like you have other kinds of relationships as well."

Realizing her mistake, George blanched.

"Oh, we do. We've dated," Wesley said quickly, taking advantage of George's shocked silence.

"We went on *one* date," she clarified. "And we didn't even make it through our entrées." Her gaze stepped carefully over to the man at her side. "We're much better coworkers than we are anything else."

Her words might've caused a less-self-assured man to lose at least a modicum of his swagger. Not Wesley. His grin became even more charming, and his pupils flared as his gaze raked over George.

Austin looked confused. Lou couldn't help but agree. She was also perplexed.

But it wasn't George whom she was having a hard time understanding. No, Lou got why George put up walls with

Wesley. She understood that even though the young woman found herself incredibly attracted to the private investigator, his handsome smirks and the arm draped across her shoulders did not fool her. George knew they were all fake.

Or were they? Lou wondered as she caught Wesley's fingers brushing lightly over the wavy locks of George's hair that were escaping her messy bun. His eyes locked on to Lou's. Seeing he'd been caught, he flicked his fingers, pretending he'd been getting rid of a piece of fuzz.

That was the part that confused Lou. During the spring, she'd been sure Wesley really, truly cared for George. His behavior any time he was around her only solidified that opinion. But in the months since their candid chat, where she'd encouraged him to talk to George about how he felt, the man hadn't done a thing. In fact, Lou was pretty sure this was the first time he and George had seen each other since their last case.

Which meant George was right. Wesley was a flirt, and he didn't care for her in that way. She was right to protect her heart, to attempt to fall out of feelings with the man.

"Well, it's great to meet you, George," Austin said, repeating his earlier sentiment. And Lou didn't miss the sparkle in his eye as he looked at her friend.

CHAPTER 6

By the time Lou made it home that evening, Marigold was already passed out on the couch in a veritable pile of multicolored yarn.

"She tried to stay awake to see you, but I think she and the rest of her bunk got about three hours of sleep the entire week at camp," Noah whispered, grinning broadly as he took in the sleeping girl.

Lou pressed her lips together to keep her laughter inside as she asked, "I'm guessing she learned to knit at camp?"

Noah chuckled. "She made you something. I haven't seen it, but for the sake of preparing you, this is what she made me." His brown eyes danced with amusement as he motioned to a "cape" she'd made him—which looked more like a small shawl.

"Where'd she get all this yarn?" Lou asked, taking in the vast amount of it piled on the couch.

"She said they gave it to her at camp." Noah shrugged. "Apparently, someone donated a bunch, and the camp kids aren't usually all that into knitting, so they were more than happy to send her home with some. But now that you've seen her, I'm going to take her up to bed."

Lou held in a giggle as Noah tried—and failed—to extricate his sleeping daughter from the yarn without making even more of a mess. Sapphy and Lilli didn't help either. The moment balls of yarn began to tumble away, the two cats appeared seemingly out of nowhere to bat them under the couch, around the coffee table, and across the room.

THE NEXT MORNING, Lou woke early so she could stop by Betsy's and Evelyn's houses, knowing she needed to water today. But when she padded into the bathroom, the gray light filtering through the frosted window and the soft patter on the roof told her it was raining for the first time in weeks. It looked like nature would do the watering for her today.

"I guess that means I have a little extra time this morning, then," she said to herself. There was no way she'd be able to go back to sleep now.

Since Noah and Marigold were still asleep, Lou crept downstairs to make herself coffee. Sapphy and Lilli were curled up together on the couch in a pile of yarn, their white fur blending, so it was hard to tell where the cat ended and the kitten started. The sight was so cute, it made Lou's heart ache. Sapphire had never minded other cats, but he'd never taken to one like this. It seemed that Lilli was just what he was looking for in a companion. Since they'd brought him home with her, he hadn't done any of his wandering and yowling, looking for the other cats at the shop.

Though she tried to be quiet, the sound of the coffee maker caused Lilli's little white head to pop up out of the pile of fur. She stretched and tumbled off the couch—along with a few balls of yarn—and trotted over to greet Lou.

"Good morning, Lillipurrtian." Lou scooped the cat into her arms, showering her warm head with kisses.

The kitten purred and kneaded her tiny claws into Lou's pajamas as Lou continued making coffee. Because the kitten only weighed a few pounds, it wasn't hard to make herself a mug of coffee while holding the animal. Then she brought her upstairs with her to sit on the balcony porch situated off the master bedroom. Lou loved sitting there because she could see into Willow's gorgeous garden, and even into the paddocks where Willow kept her horse and goat, OC and Steve. Lilli seemed to love it, too, sticking close to Lou but peering out over the expansive backyard.

Just as she took her last sip of coffee, Lou noticed an orange shape vault up onto the fence to OC's paddock next door. Willow's chestnut gelding, who'd been inside the small barn eating his morning hay, clomped out and sniffed the cat.

"Lemewl Gullipurr," Lou whispered, recognizing the cat before pulling out her phone and snapping some pictures of him with OC. The photographs would be perfect for a caption about Gullipurr meeting one of the Houyhnhms, and she knew Willow would love having OC compared to the intelligent horse race from the novel.

Checking her watch, Lou realized it was time to get everyone else up. "Want to help me?" she asked Lilli, who blinked her gorgeous blue eyes in reply. "Of course you do. It doesn't get better than waking up to a kitten."

She couldn't wait to see what her knitted gift from Marigold would be.

THE REST of the morning went smoothly, and Lou posted her pictures of Gullipurr to the blog the moment after she opened the bookshop to a waiting Silas. Luckily, he seemed in a less-than-chatty mood, so she was able to focus on the blog while he read his newspaper.

She'd just said goodbye to Silas when George arrived. She ambled over, setting her elbows on the counter in front of Lou.

"Everything okay?" Lou studied her friend. She was in yet another minuscule outfit. She'd also swept her hair up into a ponytail but had braided the part that hung down her back.

Lou didn't blame her. Even though it was raining, it was incredibly humid, making Lou wish she'd opted for a tank top herself, maybe just not one quite so small.

George sighed, wandered over to one of the bookshelves, and ran her fingertip along the spines of the books. "I've got a leak in the roof."

Wincing, Lou apologized. She and Ben had owned a condo in New York City, and the bookshop's roof was rather new, so she'd never had to deal with such an expensive repair personally. But she remembered when Willow had her roof redone last winter, and it had been an enormous expense.

"You going to see if Marty has time?" Lou asked.

Marty Spearman was the local roof guy. While many of the roofing companies in Silver Lake or Kirk used whole teams of men and got the job done in a day or two, Marty was a one-man operation and usually took a week or two to finish a job. What Marty lacked in speed, however, he made up for in quality and price. He wasn't only half the price of the bigger companies, but having your roof done by Marty was a point of pride around Button. Roofs staying intact after big storms or tree limbs falling would be followed up by someone saying, "Ah, you've got a Marty roof." That statement told them enough about the reason it held up so well.

"I've asked him." George groaned. She squinted at one of the book titles on the shelf in front of her and pulled it out. "This looks like this is in the wrong section. Anyway, you know Marty hates to work during the summer."

Lou's eyebrows lifted. She did. She'd marveled at how the man would merely wait for the frost to leave the roof each morning at Willow's before he got to work. They'd be shivering inside, warming up with cups of coffee, while he hammered away up on the roof. But Willow mentioned that he much preferred the cold to the summer heat.

"As long as it doesn't rain like this too much over the summer, I think I'll be okay. Plus, I've got to save up some more money." She opened the book that had been out of place and began flipping through the pages.

That was another thing about Marty. Being a one-man operation meant he didn't finance like the bigger companies. And although he was cheaper, it was an up-front-or-nothing kind of deal.

"Could you ask—" Lou started, but George let out a strangled sound, effectively cutting her off. "What?" Lou asked, rounding the checkout counter and craning her neck to study the book George was reading.

George's eyes were wide as they met Lou's before returning to the page. "Lou, this book is … awful." She jabbed her finger at the page.

Lou's eyes tracked across the paragraph, wincing as things became more violent and graphic.

"I thought it was odd that something so obviously horror was in the romance section," she said. "But this seems intense, even for the horror section."

Agreeing, Lou grabbed the offending book from George's grip and flipped it over to study the cover. She loved a well-written thriller. Even horror had its place in her own personal library. This? It was gratuitous. It was also not something Lou remembered purchasing. She took it over to the computer, entering the title.

"It's not in my system." Lou turned the book upside down so she wouldn't have to look at the bloody skull illustration on the cover. "I didn't buy this b—" A person entering the bookshop interrupted her statement.

Not just any person either.

Wesley St. James stopped just inside the shop as the door clicked shut behind him. His neck went taut with a swallow as his eyes landed on George, taking in her skimpier-than-normal outfit. His pupils dilated, giving a darkening effect to his blue eyes. He ran his fingers through his blond hair, but the rain meant that it spiked up in a messy, wet look.

George stood up straight, staring back at him, equally surprised.

"Hey, Wesley." Lou broke the silence, unsure whether the two of them were just going to stare at one another if she didn't. She slid the offending horror novel under the counter, planning on taking care of it later. "What can I do for you?"

Wesley's eyes flashed to Lou and then back to George, as if he couldn't look away. "I, uh—" He cleared his throat. "I actually came to see George. I went by your house, but you weren't there."

"Brilliant observation." George rolled her eyes.

"I have something to ask you." Wesley took a tentative step forward.

All the young man's swagger was gone. He seemed nervous.

Oh, gosh. Was he about to tell George how he felt? Was it just Lou, or had the air become even thicker, more humid? She wished she could back away, go hide in her office for whatever was about to happen.

He locked eyes with George. "Can I talk to you in private for a minute?"

Lou was already nodding emphatically, making escape plans, by the time George said, "Whatever you have to say to me, you can say in front of Lou." Her tone was ice cold, but Lou caught the slight tremble to it.

No, Lou wanted to protest. She really didn't want to get stuck in the middle of … whatever this was.

But Wesley swallowed again. "I came to tell you that Austin Hunt, the guy who ran that meeting yesterday, he wants to offer you a job."

Lou relaxed a little. So this wasn't about unrequited love or buried feelings. The actual topic intrigued Lou enough that she was glad she stayed.

"Then why didn't he ask me himself?" George tapped her foot.

Wesley looked down at it, clocking the movement, but then his gaze traveled up George in a way that made Lou wish, yet again, that she was in the back office.

"He... Well, he wanted me to talk to you first, t-to make sure you'd take the job."

Had Lou ever heard the suave man stammer before?

"Why wouldn't I want it?" George asked.

His attention finally roamed to her face. "Because it would mean working with me, and I told him I didn't think you would take it." His gaze dropped again, but this time to the floor.

As if there needed to be a certain amount of bravado between them, and George was picking up the slack, she cocked her hip. "What happened to us being such a good team?" She sneered, repeating his cocky sentiments from the meeting the night before.

Wesley ran his hand over the back of his neck. "I was just having fun. You know that." He glanced at Lou, then at George. "I came to tell you that if you want the job, I'll turn down my part in it. He asked for the best tech person in the area to help with surveillance, and that's you. I won't take that from you just because you don't want to work with me."

Interest softened George's rigid stance. "Surveillance? But you can set up surveillance equipment just as well as I can. Why would he need me?"

"Austin said he wants the best, and that it sounded like that's what we are … together." Wesley lifted one shoulder in an indifferent shrug. "He wants me focused on the clues and figuring out who's going to be hit next, and he wants you working on surveillance. But I think he's mostly interested in the surveillance, so I'll bow out if you want me to." He put his hands up in surrender.

George scoffed. "After all your talk yesterday, now you don't want to work with me?"

Wesley shook his head. "That's not—"

"Good, because I'm not intimidated by the idea of working with you." She lifted her chin. "You can tell Austin I'm in. I have a new roof to save for, and I need the money."

"Okay." Wesley dipped his head in what almost looked like a bow. "I'll tell him." With that, he backed toward the door. "Lou," he said with a wave.

She returned the gesture, blinking in confusion at what had just happened.

It wasn't until he'd rounded the corner and was out of sight that George collapsed back onto the counter, letting it hold up her weight.

"It just *had* to rain today?" George asked through a wail. "The man's not sexy enough dry? He had to come in here looking all damp, like some kind of Jane Austen leading man?" She let her head fall back as she shouted her questions at the ceiling of the bookstore.

Despite the tension still hanging in the space, Lou's mouth ticked up at the corner. "I didn't know you thought about the men Jane Austen wrote about."

While George was a huge fan of gaming, she wasn't

really into books unless they were of the comic or manga variety.

"I've watched the movies," she said with a snort. "The men are always the sexiest when they're wet." She began pacing. "And why was he being so nice, so … un-Wesley-like?"

Lou's mouth flattened. "Are you sure you should've said yes to working together? That kind of defeats the whole staying-away-from-him idea."

George wrinkled her nose. "It'll be fine. Staying away from him hasn't helped. If anything, it's strengthened my feelings. Maybe seeing him all the time will desensitize me to him. Plus, we'll probably just have to meet once or twice to talk about the cameras and where to set them up. After that, I can give him the log-in information and be done. And it's more money toward my roof." She clapped her hands in front of her, like she was dusting her problems off that easily.

Lou felt less sure that this plan of George's was going to work. While she and Noah had never been anything close to enemies, she remembered a similar tension living between them at one point. She'd been under the impression that he wasn't ready for another relationship, and he'd been giving her space because he thought she still hadn't moved on from her husband's death.

It hadn't been until they'd started working a case together, investigating in close quarters, that their true feelings had come through. The kiss they'd shared when the walls had finally come down was still one of the better ones of her entire life.

Maybe that was what George was hoping for. Lou sighed. Regardless of what her friend said, she hoped she knew what she was getting herself into.

CHAPTER 7

As the day progressed, it seemed George, in fact, was *not* sure about what she had gotten herself into by taking the surveillance job with Wesley.

A smattering of anxious text messages that afternoon told Lou everything she needed to know about George's deteriorating confidence surrounding her decision.

This will be fine. I'm sure of it.

That message came unprompted to Lou just after lunch. She didn't have time to respond before two more showed up.

When he said we'd have to work together, that was an overstatement. Right?

I mean, the man could probably set up his own surveillance systems, so he doesn't need me to walk him through the footage. It'll all be remote.

Lou waited a beat to make sure no more messages were incoming before answering.

> You would know better than me, but that sounds right.

Three dots appeared and then disappeared as George seemed to have a hard time deciding on what to say. While she dithered, Lou sent another message, this time to Willow.

> Free for dinner? I think George needs some support. She got herself into something I'm not sure she can handle. Might need to talk it out.

Willow responded quickly, and her incredulity was clear through the text.

> Our George? Unable to handle something? Impossible.

Their younger friend really was the definition of confidence ... usually.

> It has to do with Wesley.

That got Willow's attention.

> Say no more. I'm in. Barbecue? Bistro? Pizza?

Those were the only options downtown. Lou knew how much George enjoyed the desserts at the bistro.

Bistro. Six?

When she got the thumbs-up from Willow, Lou texted George back.

Willow and I are taking you to dinner tonight. Six. Bistro. We'll talk about it then.

Ohthankgoodness!

The text came through immediately, as if George had been hoping that was what Lou would say. She chuckled.

You know how much better I think when I've got a plate of good food in front of me.

Lou hoped it would be as simple as that.

She got a few more customers before Marigold came skipping into the shop, shucking her backpack off the moment she was through the door.

"Hey, kid," Lou said, pulling her into a tight hug. "How was school?"

Marigold sighed dramatically. "*Much* less fun than camp."

Lou chuckled. "Ah, but at least you got some good sleep last night for the first time all week."

"I could've lasted longer," Marigold muttered, but quickly moved on to her usual task of brushing the cats.

She worked independently while Lou helped a few customers, the last of which was an involved ordering process for a local book club. By the time Lou picked her head up from her computer, she caught sight of Marigold.

She'd finished with her brushing duties and had set herself up on the love seat with what looked like every ball of yarn she owned. Every cat in the shop perched on a part of the sofa, watching the yarn with a predatory focus.

Lou wasn't sure whether to laugh or cry at the sight. She opened her mouth, but before she could get any words of warning out, Jane Pawsten made the first move. She pounced on one of the yarn balls, grabbing it with her teeth and galloping away. The weight of her jumping onto the cushion sent three other yarn balls flying into the air and rolling across the shop. Clawrcy and Charles Lickens batted at the yarn, sending even more rolling away.

Marigold chortled in response and Lou couldn't help but join in on the laughter.

"Do you have any schoolbooks in your backpack, or was it just chock-full of yarn?" Lou let out an exasperated chuckle. As far as she could tell, all the yarn from last night was still at their house, draped across the couch. Where the child had gotten more, Lou wasn't sure.

"Mrs. Yellowlees had a bunch of yarn in her art cabinet that had just been sitting there, so she said I could have it," Marigold explained innocently.

Together they cleaned up the yarn, but Lou had a sneaking suspicion they'd missed a few balls of it since there was still room in her backpack when they zipped the thing closed.

By the time Cassidy came to pick Marigold up, and the end of business hours rolled around, Lou had almost forgotten about the creepy horror novel George had found earlier. It caught her eye, however, when she went to grab a bag from under the counter.

Once her customer left, and Lou was in the bookshop alone, she pulled the book out and studied it more closely. Along with a summary and barcode on the back cover, there was a website listed for the author. Lou typed it into her browser, and a website for R. G. Stillhouse pulled up. Befitting the dark book the author had written, the site was both dark and bloody. She shivered a little, clicking on the section of the website dedicated to telling her about the author.

A picture of a man wearing a cowboy hat loaded. But other than learning that the author had always had a penchant for horror movies and books, she didn't learn much about him.

Chewing on her lip for a moment, Lou picked up her phone and searched the internet for bookstores in Silver Lake. While she *could've* called Austin to talk to him, Lou needed the expertise of someone who'd been in the book buying and selling business for a while. She needed a veteran, and Austin was even newer than she was.

The shop she was looking for came up as the second option. She entered the number on her phone and pressed the call button.

"Used books. This is Lance." The man's distracted voice carried through the phone speaker. If Lou had to guess, he was reading and wasn't going to put the book down for something as unimportant as a phone call.

"Hi, Lance. It's Louisa Henry from Button Books. Well, Whiskers and Words, now."

There was a beat of silence. Her last interaction with Lance Swatek hadn't been quite as bad as the one with

Rupert from Silver Lake Books, but he also didn't seem excited to hear from her.

"Right. Cats and books. People either love your place or hate it," he finally said.

Lou grunted out a laugh. "Sounds about right."

"What can I do for you, Louisa Henry?"

Her attention slipped back to the mysterious book in her care. "I'm calling with a bit of a mystery. I was wondering if you've ever had anything like this happen."

"Intriguing," he said. "Shoot."

"Well, I found a book on my shelves today that I didn't purchase." She made sure to make that distinction because while the *Gulliver's Travels* books were mysteriously appearing on her shelves, at least she'd ordered those.

"In your used section?" Lance asked.

"No, actually. It was in my romance section, but it's definitely not romance." She snorted, remembering the paragraph she'd read. No one who wrote about terrible things like that happening to a woman was writing a love story.

Lance paused. "Does it have a bloody skull on the cover?"

With a sharp intake of breath, Lou said, "Yes. How did you know?"

A tired laugh escaped the used bookseller. "The author's local. He keeps trying to get us to sell his book. He made the mistake of going to Eloise first."

A shiver moved through Lou at the reminder of the other used bookseller in Silver Lake. There was a reason Lou had called Lance instead of Eloise. The older woman might appear harmless, but she was cutthroat.

"I'm guessing that didn't go well," Lou scoffed.

"She took one look inside, said it was too violent, and told him she wouldn't carry it," Lance explained. "Eloise had already warned me by the time he showed up at my place. I told him he could leave a copy here, but if it didn't sell in sixty days, he needed to either come get it, or I was going to toss it in the trash." Lou could picture Lance shrugging after that comment.

"I guess he just skipped the whole asking-me part," Lou mused, frowning down at the book.

"He was probably hoping you'd sell a copy and ask him for more. Look inside the front cover."

Lou did. Inside was a handwritten note in what looked like something that could only be described as a serial killer's handwriting. "If a customer wants to buy this copy, charge what you want for it and keep the profit on me. All I ask is that you email me to order more," she read the note aloud. "And then he included his email address. Ew."

"Yeaaah."

"Have you had anyone interested in buying the copy he left you?"

"Oh, absolutely not," Lance said with another dry, one-note laugh. "It's far too gratuitously violent for even my most devout horror readers."

There was a shuffling sound in the background, and Lou could tell Lance was taking off his worn baseball cap to scratch at his hair before placing his hat back on his head. It was a habit he had—one that got worse when he was lying, but Lou had a feeling he was telling the truth here.

"Hmmm. Okay, well, thanks anyway."

"No problem. See you around, Lou." And with that, Lance hung up.

Lou considered doing just what Lance had mentioned to the author if his book didn't sell, eyeing the garbage to her right. But as much as she would have loved to never have to look at the words on its pages ever again, the fact that it had been put here, in her shop, without her permission, during a time when that was also happening with the *Gulliver's Travels* copies, felt too coincidental. She stashed it behind the checkout counter and moved on to her closing chores.

Lou had just locked the bookshop's front door, corralled the cats upstairs to the apartment, and was about to leave for dinner when the glint of gold lettering caught her eye in the science fiction section. While gilt lettering wasn't uncommon in a bookstore, science fiction covers tended to be more modern, moving away from the classic book-binding techniques.

Lou wandered over to the section. Her pulse pounded in her eardrums as she recognized the book.

It was a special illustrated hardback edition of *Gulliver's Travels.*

Discomfort crawled up the backs of her arms on spider legs. She shuddered off the feeling as she reached for the book, plucking it from the shelf.

"This is number six," Lou said aloud in the quiet space. "Are they going to slowly return all twenty-four of them to me?"

It was the oddest form of thievery she'd ever encountered.

She was about to turn on her heel, placing the book with the rest of the ones that had been returned, when she realized there was a paper sticking out of the top. A bookmark? Sliding the thing out, Lou found a note-card-sized piece of paper. On it, a paragraph had been typed by what looked to be an authentic typewriter—if the smudges of ink and misalignments were anything to go by. Certain letters jogged down slightly, not in line with the rest.

The sun burned in
the sky, burned a
hole right
through it.
The sky was a
piece of blue
paper and the sun
a beam of light
bouncing off a
magnifying glass,
burning through,
burning
everything. 20:00

There was something about the prose that felt familiar, but Lou couldn't figure out where it was from. She took the page over to the checkout counter and pulled the other five books from where she'd been hiding them. Paging through each one, she searched for a similar piece of paper, but found none.

This was the only one with a confusingly typed bookmark. Studying the text, she turned to her computer and pulled up a few of her favorite plagiarism detectors from her old life as an editor in New York City. Whenever a line or paragraph felt too familiar while she was editing, she'd pop it into one of these programs to make sure it hadn't been lifted from another piece of writing.

But each search came up empty.

Wherever this paragraph had come from, it wasn't from a published book or article.

She was still studying it, trying to figure out what it meant, and why it was so poorly typed out, when there was a knock on the glass. Lou jumped, only to see Willow and George standing out front, waiting for her.

Lou shoved the page in her purse, set the newest copy of *Gulliver's Travels* on the stack of others she kept behind the counter, and then she joined her friends.

While the rain had stopped, gray clouds still hung low in the sky, giving the air a bite to it that had the three women rushing to the bistro. Their server sat them at one of the coveted window tables, and they ordered immediately, knowing exactly what they wanted without needing to peruse the menu.

"So…" Willow glanced between Lou and George. "What's wrong with George?"

The younger woman released a loaded breath. "Where do I start?"

Willow belted out a laugh. "I mean, what has you freaking out today, specifically?"

"She agreed to work with Wesley on the surveillance systems for the anti-thievery job Austin introduced at the meeting last night," Lou explained.

George held up a finger. "In my defense, I need the money. I found a leak in my roof."

Willow narrowed her eyes as she took in the information. "Wesley asked you to work with him?"

Snorting, George replied, "No. He said Austin approached him after the meeting last night, saying he 'wanted the best,' and it sounded like that's what we were, together." Her voice caught on the last word. She coughed. "But I think Wesley's little joke went too far. He didn't expect Austin to take his whole 'we make a great team' speech so seriously."

"How do you know it was a joke?" Willow pursed her lips.

"Because when he offered me the job, he said he'd step down and let me have it," George answered matter-of-factly. "He clearly didn't want to work with me if he could help it."

Willow's eyes contracted slightly. "Didn't he?"

"Ask Lou." George motioned across the table. "She was there. She saw how he was."

Lou swallowed, buying herself some time to calculate her response. To her, it had seemed like Wesley recognized that he'd gotten them into that situation and wanted to give George an easy out. He'd also appeared to be sad about the prospect that George might not want him around. Again, she wondered if that was actually the man's motivation or if she was assigning emotions to him because that's what she wanted him to feel for George.

"Lou, tell her." George's tone wavered with a hint of panic. She'd obviously expected Lou to jump to her defense, and the hesitation had caused her certainty to fray. "Everything's a joke to Wesley. It's why we won't work."

Grasping on to the desperation in her friend's voice, Lou said, "Right. I think it might be good for you to go through all the reasons you and Wesley aren't right. That way, if you have to see one another throughout this project, you'll be able to fall back on those reasons."

"Even when he runs a hand through his hair?" George asked with a whimper.

"Remind yourself that you hate how you never know if he's being serious or not," Willow supplied, using the most recent example George had given.

A modicum of the tension in George's shoulders loosened. "Right. That is frustrating." A smile curled her lips as her confidence returned. "And what if he leans against a doorframe—with his arm like this?" She mimed reaching up and resting her arm against an invisible entryway. A bit of panic returned to her eyes as they locked on to Lou.

"You remind yourself that you value open communication," Lou supplied for her.

George's lips twisted downward. "And if he speaks in riddles that make me think he's interested in me?"

"Think of Geralt," Willow blurted.

Lou nodded. "Yes, Geralt is your favorite thing in the world, and Wesley doesn't like cats."

"Oh, that's good." George snapped her fingers. "Should I be writing these down?"

Lou reached into her bag, her fingers grazing the edge of the paper she'd found in the most recently returned book. But instead of searching for a pen, George pulled out her phone and started a new note. Feeling silly, Lou extracted her fingers from her purse, but she couldn't help letting her thoughts and gaze linger on the note for a second or two.

"Poor communication, never know when he's serious, hates my cat," George murmured as she typed out the reasons they'd already discussed. Her gaze lifted to her friends. "What about how he makes me feel like I'm on fire?"

Lou and Willow exchanged fleeting glances.

Willow coughed. "In a good way?"

George went rigid. "Is it ever good to be on fire?"

Tilting her head to one side, Willow said, "I mean…"

George drew in a thoughtful breath, looking at Lou.

"On fire, in the metaphorical sense, can definitely feel good," Lou admitted. Then, at George's panicked expression, Lou added, "But obviously not the way Wesley makes you feel."

It didn't matter how compatible she thought the two of them might be. If George didn't want to be with Wesley, Lou was going to support her in that.

George's mention of fire, however, brought Lou's mind back to the odd paragraph typewritten on the paper in her purse. She glanced down at it once more just as their dinner arrived. As they ate, they continued to list reasons George might use to maintain distance from Wesley if they found their paths crossing while doing surveillance on the case.

They'd just ordered dessert when George said, "I can't believe there have already been five burglaries. Well, six if you count yours, Lou."

"Five burglaries. Five books," Lou whispered to herself.

"Huh?" Willow asked, leaning closer.

"Don't you think it's odd that there have been the same number of books that have shown back at my shop?" Lou blinked, her gaze moving again to the note in her purse—the one found in the sixth book returned after they'd been stolen from her shop. "Well, actually, I guess that's not true anymore."

"Why not?" George sat back as the server brought their desserts.

They each dug in, Lou taking a bite before she answered.

"I found a sixth one today." Her eyes moved to the note. "This one had something in it."

"Is that what you've been staring at all evening?" George craned her neck to see inside Lou's purse.

Willow clicked her tongue. "Yeah, you keep reaching in there to touch something, as if you're worried it's going to disappear. What's going on?"

Sighing, Lou pulled out the paper and explained where she'd found it.

As she stared, however, what had at first presented as random typewriter keys out of alignment suddenly jumped out at her as a code.

"Look," she said, pointing to the page. "There's an 'r that's below the line here, but not over here."

The sun burned in
the sky, burned a
hole right
through it.
The sky was a
piece of blue
paper and the sun
a beam of light
bouncing off a
magnifying glass,
burning through,
burning
everything. 20:00

"If the type bar was really out of alignment, it wouldn't only do this randomly. This has to be a clue."

Pulling out a pen from her purse, Lou circled each of the letters sitting below the line, then she rewrote them below, putting spaces between as words formed.

The sun burned in
the sky, burned a
hole right
through it.
The sky was a
piece of blue
paper and the sun
a beam of light
bouncing off a
magnifying glass,
burning through,
burning
everything. 20:00

brine art supply 20:00

"Brine art supply twenty-hundred hours." Lou glanced up and met Willow and George in the eyes. "I think the art store is going to be the next place that the thieves hit."

CHAPTER 8

Willow was on the phone with Easton before Lou and George could even settle their bill. They joined her outside, waiting for her to finish her call.

"Okay. See you soon." Willow hung up, turning toward her friends. "He's coming to talk. I told him we'd meet at the bookshop."

"Sure." Lou led the way back through the alley to the bookshop.

She let her friends inside and started some hot water for tea in her office. They were just settling around the seating area in the middle of the bookshop with steaming mugs when Easton pulled up and knocked on the front door. He wore a T-shirt and shorts instead of his usual suit, proving he'd already gone home after work.

Willow jogged over, stretching on her tiptoes to plant a kiss on his cheek the moment she opened the door for him.

Easton's lips tipped up into a roguish smirk. Instead of walking past Willow, however, he wrapped his arms around her and dipped her into a deeper kiss. She squealed happily. George looked like she wanted to poke her eyes out, but Lou just gazed in adoration at her happy friends.

Back on her feet, Willow grabbed on to Easton's T-shirt and buried her face into his shoulder. She pulled in a deep sniff.

"You smell like horse," Willow said with a reverence most people reserved for expensive colognes or fragrant flowers. She took another whiff as Easton chuckled.

"I was doing a little weeding in the backyard and the troublemaker was trying to help." There was a lightness to Easton's tone that conveyed the love he had for Willow's horse.

Named after the *Mr. Ed* theme song, OC—Of Course— might not have been able to talk, but he got into as many situations as the sitcom star from the hit show. Hence Easton's nickname for the animal: troublemaker.

"Actually, that's a lie," Easton amended. "OC and I mainly watched while Steve did all the weeding." Without prompting, Easton shook his head. "That's also not true. I think Steve ate more plants we wanted to keep than he did weeds." The detective cringed as he admitted as much.

Steve, their pygmy goat, was probably more deserving of the troublemaker nickname. But everyone thought he was too adorable to find whatever he did anything other than charming.

The lightness surrounding the happy couple flattened as they sank onto the love seat together, and Easton looked at Lou.

"Okay, so what's this big revelation Willow told me you had?"

Lou handed him the piece of paper. "I found another book, and this was sticking out the top." She didn't say more than that, letting him read the paragraph and her scribbled translation of the code below.

But the note was not as self-explanatory as Lou had expected, because Easton merely squinted at the page and then squeezed his eyes shut in a long blink. "Sorry, but it's been a long day. Do you mind telling me what I'm supposed to find interesting about the art store in Brine at eight o'clock?"

Willow laid a hand on Easton's knee. "Five businesses have been robbed or burglarized. Lou's found five returned books in her shop. She's wondering if there's a link between those two things."

Lou took over the story. "This book is number six, but none of the others have had a piece of paper inside. I checked. Easton, what if this is the next place that's going to be hit?"

Confusion turned to intrigue as Easton considered the possibility. He studied the paper in front of him a second time with more interest.

"You think they're going to hit the art store in Brine at eight o'clock tonight?" Easton summarized.

"Or tomorrow," George chimed in.

Lou's phone buzzed, and she checked the message, allowing Easton time to think. It was a text from Noah.

> Saw the camera notification go off after hours at the shop. Then I noticed it was you. Everything okay?

I think so. I found another book. I think they might be connected to the thefts. I'm showing Easton now and then I'll be home.

Noah gave her message a thumbs-up. Her heart warmed that he was helping her check the camera notifications like he said he would.

Easton stood. "I'm going to get on the phone with the Brine PD and give them a heads-up." He placed a kiss on Willow's forehead, then he moved toward the front of the bookstore to make the call.

Before he could get more than a few feet away, Easton tripped on a ball of yarn that must have rolled out from under a shelf somewhere.

"Wh-what is that?" Easton froze, holding his right foot up as he peered down at what he'd tripped on. Eyelids sinking closed in relief, he said, "Oh, good. It's just yarn. I thought I'd stepped on that new kitten of yours."

"Oh, sorry." Lou jumped up to grab the rogue ball of yarn. "Lilli's at our place, remember? For this very reason. She probably would be underfoot." She wound the loose yarn around itself and tucked it away. "This is from Marigold. She visited me earlier after school. Apparently, she really got into knitting during fifth-grade camp last week, and she's got yarn coming out of her sleeves. I thought we'd found all of it, but the cats must've stashed this one away."

Easton eyed the offending craft. "I don't envy you and Noah that hobby."

Lou shrugged. "She made me a scarf." It had been

lopsided, three different colors, and only about two feet long, but Lou loved it.

She stashed the yarn behind the counter where it wouldn't accidentally roll out again, before returning to the seating area. As Easton talked to his fellow officers, Lou felt a weight lift off her shoulders. She glanced at George and then Willow, noting that the evening clouds had parted, and sunshine now streamed through the bookshop windows.

"Drinks on our deck?" Lou asked, not wanting the time with her friends to end.

George rubbed her hands together. "Oh, I'm in, especially since my first meeting with Austin and Wesley is on Wednesday afternoon. I might as well enjoy my time before I begin this job."

"I don't know if I can make the trek," Willow said, the sarcasm in her tone clear and a grin already pulling across her face before she could even get the full sentence out. She snorted out a laugh. "Of course."

Easton rejoined the group, giving them a nod of confirmation. "They're going to set up patrols around the building right now." He let out a sigh much like the one Lou had just released.

They told him about drinks on Noah and Lou's back deck, and his smile widened even further. George hopped in the car with Lou, citing the preference to walk home later, and before long, they were all seated in the cushy outdoor furniture, watching the sun lower in the sky. Ice from the drinks Noah made them clinked as they sipped contentedly, the delicate sound occasionally punctuated by a snort from OC as he monitored them from his paddock.

"You know, Noah and I have talked about taking down that fence to make this part of the backyard into a field turnout for OC." Lou waved at the meadow behind their garden.

Willow scoffed. "He'd love that. But are you sure you'd want to give up that space?"

Lou placed a hand on her chest. "Only the best for my nephew. Plus, even if we did, we'd still have room for Mom and Dad to park their RV over there." She gestured to the level area that ran perpendicular to Spool Avenue but was hidden behind trees to give them some privacy.

"It's a lovely dream, Lou," Willow said wistfully.

It was absolutely the perfect temperature. They were sitting with friends, sipping on delicious cocktails on their deck while the police waited to possibly apprehend the people who'd been terrorizing the northern section of Lakeside County. *Life was good*, Lou thought to herself.

She glanced at her watch, then at Easton, noting that he, too, was checking his phone to see if there were any updates. It was closing in on eight o'clock.

A phone buzzed with an incoming message. But it wasn't Easton's. Lou and Noah glanced down to see a message come through from Cassidy. It was on the group chat they used for the three of them to organize pickup and drop-off schedules for Marigold, and it only consisted of four words.

We need to talk.

Fear clutched at Lou's throat, and her gaze snapped up

to meet Noah's. Her significant other wore a similarly terrified expression.

"Why do the two of you look like you just simultaneously swallowed bugs?" George asked, breaking the silence.

The column of Noah's throat tensed as he swallowed. "Uh, Cass just texted that she needs to talk to us."

As if prompted by his mention of her, another message came through.

I'm done. I can't do this.

Lou choked on the sip she'd been taking of her drink, the one she'd taken to soothe the closed-up feeling in her airway. "This is bad," she whispered.

"Should we leave?" Willow asked, sitting forward from the reclined position she'd been lounging in. "George can come with us if Cass needs to come here and talk to you."

Noah grunted out a noncommittal sound as he reread the message.

"What could she be upset about?" Lou asked, trying to rack her brain for anything that had gone remotely wrong over the past week.

Honestly, she couldn't think of a thing. Noah and Cassidy were a well-oiled coparenting machine at that point, and the addition of Lou had only made things easier. She'd merely become one more responsible adult added to the mix of people who could pick up, drop off, or take care of Marigold. But maybe that was the exact problem. Maybe the addition of Lou had created an issue they hadn't seen because they wanted so badly for everything to work out.

Lou's mind didn't even get to finish its rapid descent into anxiety because another message came through from Cassidy. This time, the message was a picture, not a text.

The photograph was of Cassidy's fancy white sofa, completely covered in a web of different colored yarns. It was followed by a crying-laughing emoji.

Noah's deep laugh rang out through the tense silence that had accumulated during the tense seconds it had taken Cassidy to respond.

"What?" Willow asked.

George leaned forward, trying to see Lou's phone.

"It's Marigold's yarn. It's everywhere," Lou explained with a burst of air, unable to hold back her relief. "It must've taken the photo longer to send than the texts," she added, giggling as Noah continued to chuckle.

"Oh, I agree with Cassidy. The stuff is all over the book-shop, too, and the little munchkin has only been home for a day." George shook her head, but she wore a smirk.

Noah began typing a response. "I'm telling her our house looks even worse." He sent the message.

Another text buzzed through, but it wasn't Noah or Lou's phones.

This time, it was Easton's. He snatched his device from the tabletop, eyes moving across the screen. Taking a hard swallow before glancing up, he said, "They didn't see any signs of the thieves at the art shop in Brine, and it's half past. They're going to wait longer, but they don't feel confi-dent the hit was happening tonight."

"Will they wait tomorrow too?" Willow asked.

Easton nodded. "Fingers crossed it was meant for tomorrow."

Because the alternative was that Lou had just made up the connection between the books and the burglaries. She sipped the last of her drink, but somehow it didn't taste as sweet.

EASTON STOPPED by the next evening to let Lou know the thieves hadn't shown that night either.

"They're going to keep a detail on the store for the next few evenings," Easton explained, "but I think it's safe to say that the note left in the book was unrelated."

Lou conceded the same. Hoping to get things headed back to her normal rhythm, Lou ran to work the next morning, stopping one last time at both Evelyn's and Betsy's homes since the two women were set to return sometime today.

Summer tourists kept Lou running after she opened the bookshop, but things settled down just after lunch, just in time for Betsy and Evelyn to show. Taking advantage of the empty store, Lou locked up and placed a sign in the door, telling customers she would reopen shortly, so she could chat with the two travelers about their trip.

She ushered them over to the seating area and produced the spare keys to their respective houses.

"Mail piles are each on the kitchen counters, and as far as I can tell, all your plants are thriving."

The women thanked her yet again and began gushing about their trip. The trip details only lasted so long, however, before the conversation moved to Lou's *Gullipurr's Travels* blog.

"I think we missed home a little more than we were willing to let on," Evelyn admitted as she sipped on the tea Lou had made her. "But your blog was the perfect way for us to feel like we were staying connected."

Betsy beamed. "We checked your site every day, making predictions about what that little rascal would be up to each time."

"Though we don't know the story, so we weren't able to predict very well." Evelyn pursed her lips. "Or pronounce any of the names, especially those smart horses."

"You haven't read it?" Lou asked Evelyn, slightly aghast. The woman had been a high school librarian for her entire career.

"I'm embarrassed to admit that I haven't," Evelyn said, cheeks reddening.

Betsy snapped her fingers. "Which was why we were going to remember to pick up a couple copies today." She craned her neck, searching the store for a display of the books.

Lou winced. "Actually, that's something I didn't put on the blog, but we've had some trouble with thefts lately." She gave them a summary of the goings-on over the past few weeks, including the sad news about Heather.

She kept the news of the books returning to herself. While she technically could've sold the ones she'd gotten back—she'd purchased them fair and square, after all—something didn't feel right. They might not be connected with the robberies like she thought, but Lou had a feeling there was something tying them to the local thefts, and she didn't want to let them out of her sight just yet.

"Anyway." Lou bounced her shoulders. "Those special

editions I ordered were stolen, but I have a replacement order on the way."

Betsy's mouth narrowed in defiance. "That can't be right. I swear I just saw one around here… Yes." The older woman's plaited hair swung as she turned her attention to the shelf of gardening books next to the seating area. "Isn't that one?" She pointed.

Lou and Evelyn got up and scrambled over to where Betsy indicated.

Sure enough, there sat one of the very same copies the men had stolen from Lou weeks earlier. And the book had a piece of paper sticking out the top, just like the one the other day.

CHAPTER 9

Lou's fingers trembled as she pulled the paper out of the book. Her eyes slid over the lines of typewritten text.

He grabbed her
wrist.
"No," she
cried. "Let go
of me!"
But he knew
she didn't
mean it. He
pulled her
closer.
"I'm serious.
I don't love
you," she
protested.
He scoffed.
She was just
playing hard to
get.
23:00

Lou pulled a face at the text. It seemed like a negative example from a human resources training course about consent. She had the overwhelming urge to scream, *No means no!* at the paper. But then something caught her eye. Just as with the last one, certain letters were typed lower than others.

"What's that?"

Lou jumped at the sound of Evelyn's gruff voice. She'd completely forgotten that the women were still there. She itched to grab a pen and figure out what the code said.

"It's a bit of a puzzle, actually," Lou admitted.

She looked over at the two women. Their postures were relaxed, practically lazy compared to the bunched-up feeling of tension winding through Lou's limbs. They also didn't move to leave, obviously not planning on going anywhere soon, which was a problem. Lou needed some time by herself to figure this out.

"Um, I forgot that I have an appointment with … George," Lou lied. "She's helping me with my computer and—"

"Oh! I'd love to see her." Betsy craned her neck toward the front door.

Lou had forgotten that Betsy had likely been George's bus driver back during her school days. "I'm actually going to her," she said quickly.

Evelyn and Betsy narrowed their eyes. Their gazes tiptoed over to the large desktop computer on Lou's checkout counter, rightly wondering why she would travel to George with the machine when the woman could come here.

"She has some special equipment at her place." Lou hoped the two women, who weren't the techiest of sorts, wouldn't question what that equipment might be.

Betsy stared meaningfully at the hardback still gripped in Lou's hands.

"I'll let you know when the new ones come in," she said, clutching it tighter to her body.

That satisfied the women, and they finally left. Once they were gone, Lou relocked the door behind them, raced over to the table, and pulled out a notepad. She circled the letters before rewriting the message below.

He grabbed her
wrist.
"No," she
cried. "Let go
of me!"
But he knew
she didn't
mean it. He
pulled her
closer.
"I'm serious.
I don't love
you," she
protested.
He scoffed.
She was just
playing hard to
get.
23:00

button up 23:00

Button Up was the local outdoor equipment store. Twenty-three hundred. Eleven o'clock at night. Was the outdoor store the next to be hit?

Lou pulled out her phone and called Easton.

"Hey," he said conversationally.

"I found another book. It has another note in it." She dispensed with pleasantries, cutting to the important part. "The message says Button Up is going to be hit at eleven o'clock at night. Do you want me to bring it in so you can see it?"

Lou vaguely wondered if the thieves might've left any fingerprints on the book, though she'd all but ruined those with the way she was gripping it. She'd have to remember that for the next time she found one.

"I could use a walk. I'll come to you." The sound of chair wheels rolling in the background told Lou he was getting up from his desk.

"See you soon," Lou said before hanging up.

She scanned the street through the front window, wishing she'd kept an eye on where Betsy and Evelyn had gone. If they were sitting in the café across the street, she didn't want them to see her staying put when she'd shooed them out under the pretense of meeting with George. She supposed that if they asked, she could come clean.

Lou paced. Suddenly, something tangled around her feet, and she looked down to see more yarn.

"I was right. We definitely didn't find it all the other day." Lou groaned in frustration.

She spent the next few minutes following the yarn to the

source and searching for any more hiding beneath book-shelves.

When Easton arrived a few minutes later, Lou shoved the paper toward him, waiting as he studied it.

The tendons in his neck tightened as he swallowed. "Okay. I'll set up a team to watch the place tonight." He flipped the paper over and then right side up again. "I noticed a pattern today. Ever since your bookstore was robbed, these have been happening at three-day intervals. If the pattern had continued, some place should have been hit last night, Tuesday. But it was the first time in almost two weeks that there wasn't a business hit in Brine, Button, or Silver Lake on that schedule."

Lou's eyebrows arched higher on her forehead. "Are they moving to Tinsdale or Kirk?" She couldn't imagine what thieves might want in Tinsdale. The place was practically a ghost town. But Kirk was huge, boasting twice the population of Silver Lake, and home to a lot of big-box stores.

"Nope. Neither of them reported any issues either." His blue eyes shifted as he thought.

As if she could read his thoughts, Lou said, "The other books I found didn't have papers in them by the time I looked through them."

Easton's eyes sparkled with the excitement brought on by the same revelation. "You removed the paper from the book on Tuesday, which meant that the person who was supposed to come get the location and time never could."

Their gazes locked in a simultaneous decision.

"We have to put the paper back so the thief can come get the information," Lou said with a gasp.

"And then I'll be waiting to arrest them the moment they attempt to break into Button Up"—Easton counted—"Friday evening. That's three days from when the last theft was supposed to take place."

"But you'll still watch tonight and tomorrow, right?" Lou asked.

"Just in case." Easton ducked his chin.

Chest rising and falling quickly, Lou paced. "Okay. I guess I'll put this back where it was and … supervise anyone who comes in to look." She stopped short. "If I catch the person, should I confront them? Try to keep them here?"

Easton frowned. "No, don't engage. They're not technically doing anything illegal, and you could easily get the wrong person. It's possible whoever comes to get the times or drops off the books isn't fully aware of what they're involved in."

"Right. They could be pawns." Lou hated that she felt such relief at being given the okay not to approach the person, whomever it may be.

Plan in place, Easton left Lou to reshelve the book and carry on with her day as she normally would.

"Normal" turned out to be an elusive state of being for Lou to achieve the rest of the afternoon. After returning the book to the shelf Betsy had plucked it from, paper sitting in the same halfway position inside, Lou entirely forgot how to act.

She greeted customers either too enthusiastically or not

at all, forgetting to speak in lieu of documenting everything about them in case they turned out to be there for the illicit paper. She wandered through the aisles, trying to catch a glimpse of anyone who went near the book.

Based on the awkward stares, the tight sets to customers' shoulders, and multiple patrons leaving without buying a thing, Lou's "normal" behavior was scaring people away.

She tried a different tactic closer to the end of the day. She hid in the office, pretending to be in the middle of a task, and therefore removing herself from the front of the shop altogether. It was a risky venture, given that she'd been robbed just weeks earlier, and the plan left the store quite vulnerable. But she had the cameras to look back on if anything happened. Lou fed the cats an early dinner, luring them all into the back room just in case.

So, that was where Lou was, hiding in her back office, when the bell on the front door rang. Stiffening, Lou quieted her breathing and resisted the urge to call out a greeting. She wanted to try not saying anything at all, to see what someone did if they thought they were alone inside the shop.

Measured footsteps sounded in the shop as the person ventured farther inside. Lou could just picture the movement that matched with such a rhythm. Step, glance, step, scan, step, search. This was an inquisitive customer, and they were trying to locate her. Heart rate skyrocketing in the suspense, Lou peered through the small sliver she could see through between the door and the frame.

She just caught the back of someone walking toward the gardening section, toward the book, when...

"Lou? Are you here?" George's voice rang out in the quiet, shattering the tension.

She closed her eyes. It was only George. "In the back," she called. "I'll be right out."

George grumbled something that Lou didn't catch. While the exact words had eluded her, George's tone was obvious—she was unnerved, possibly even upset. It was then that Lou remembered George had her initial meeting with Austin and Wesley that afternoon. Had something gone wrong? Did George need to vent to her?

Rushing out of the office, Lou said, "Oh! How was the meeting? Did our plan wo—"

"The meeting went fine," George called out in a tight, rushed sort of voice, cutting Lou off before she could finish.

As Lou rounded a bookshelf, and the seating area came into view, she understood why. Wesley stood in the middle of the shop, hands tucked nonchalantly into the pockets of the gray khaki shorts he wore. Well, he also wore a self-satisfied grin, as if he knew exactly what Lou had been about to say. George, hair braided in twin French braids and wearing a summery sundress, was sporting her embarrassment in a red blotch on her chest and neck, fully visible thanks to the low neckline of her dress.

"Hi, Wesley." Lou coughed to hide her embarrassment.

George glanced behind Lou. "What were you doing back there?"

"Hiding," Lou admitted with a snort.

At George's familiar voice, the cats trotted out of the office, joining them in the middle of the bookshop. Lou gestured for Wesley and George to sit, and she told them everything about the most recent book she'd found and how she and Easton were hoping to set a trap.

Wesley nodded, impressed. "I can't say I would've figured it out as quickly as you two did, but I hope it works." His humble admission surprised Lou, but then he followed it up with, "Then 'Gorge' and I wouldn't even have to go through all the trouble of setting up the surveillance points."

George stiffened where she sat, petting Anne Mice.

"I'm sorry. Did you just call her *Gorge*?" Lou frowned at the unflattering departure from her friend's name.

George let out a preemptive groan.

Wetting his lips first, Wesley's teeth flashed in an almost feral grin. "Why, yes. I did. Thank you for asking, Lou." His gaze flicked over to George. "That's what Austin Hunt called her about a dozen times during our meeting. Well, he called her Gorgeous George first a few times before just shortening it to Gorge."

Lou's eyebrows shot up. "During your meeting?" It felt a little unprofessional to Lou, but she also wasn't a single young adult anymore. Maybe it was less frowned upon to flirt in business meetings than it used to be.

George let her head fall back onto the couch and squeezed her eyes shut.

Seeing that she wasn't going to do any of the talking, Wesley happily picked up the slack. "I'd say our new acquaintance, Austin, has a crush on our girl."

The girl in question froze, her fingers stilling in the middle of a stroke of Annie's fur. Lou thought it was probably the surprise of hearing Wesley call her "our girl," as if claiming her. But after a moment to buffer, George found her voice.

"He does not have a crush. He was a little flirty. That was all. There's nothing there." George's tone was sharp, brokering no argument.

Wesley held up his hands, but his eyes sparked with joy and something else Lou thought might be jealousy.

"So, what else happened at your meeting?" Lou asked, wondering what had gone awry. If things had gone according to George's plan, her time spent with Wesley should have been over with after the meeting.

At that, George and Wesley swapped exasperated glances.

"Austin insisted that I be the only one with access to the video files," George admitted with a sigh. "If Wesley wants to look through the footage, we have to do that together. Unfortunately," she added, with a glower at the man across from her.

Wesley rolled his eyes, but it seemed to be directed at Austin instead of George because he followed up the movement by saying, "The guy's more paranoid than a scientist in a movie where the world's about to end. But I guess I would be, too, if my aspirations to become the president of the Silver Lake Chamber of Commerce hinged on catching these thieves." He jerked one shoulder up, then let it fall. "Which is actually why we're here." Wesley looked around.

"Oh. Right." George straightened her posture. "We were hoping to find Easton. When we stopped by the station, Reynolds said he'd come here and hadn't been back since."

Lou blinked in understanding. "He's probably at Button Up, to be honest. He was going to talk to Michelle when we parted ways. I think he was going to scope out where the thieves might try to break in."

Scooting Anne Mice off her lap, George stood. "Great. Thanks." She jerked her head toward the door. "Come on, St. James. Let's get this over with."

"I'd follow you anywhere, Gorge." Wesley waggled his eyebrows rakishly, and then pushed off the sofa, trailing behind her.

Lou chuckled as they left, not sure if Austin Hunt knew what he was getting himself into by pairing the two of them together.

CHAPTER 10

L ou was just about to go home for the evening when Willow pulled up in front of the bookstore in her truck. She still wore the gardening gloves she had on most days while working at the nursery, and there was a pair of pruning shears in her hand as she slid out of the driver's seat.

"Hey." Lou put on her sunglasses to combat the evening sunshine. "Do you need me to open back up?" She jerked her thumb toward the front door she'd just locked behind her.

"Nope. Just wanted to check on the smoke bushes and make sure they didn't need pruning." Willow tilted her head to one side, then the other, as she appraised the magenta-colored bushes with the fluffy pink flowers.

"Oh, good. You're still here," George said as she jogged up to them on the sidewalk.

"Hey, George," Willow called from halfway inside the plant.

"Actually, she goes by 'Gorge' now." Lou shot the young woman a teasing look.

Willow extricated herself from the plant, making a sour face. "Why?"

George grimaced. "*Ugh*. Not you too," she said to Lou. "It's been a long day, and if you tease me, I won't tell you about my big news."

"Fair enough." Laughing, Lou unlocked the door to the bookshop and ushered them both inside.

They settled around the front table, Willow still eyeing the plants out front, impatient to get back to work.

"Okay, so what's the big news?" Willow asked. "And why do you have a new name?"

George settled her elbows on the table and then propped her chin on the heels of her hands. "Gorge is what Austin called me all throughout our meeting today." She pulled an exasperated face, but the grin that took over after showed how much she actually enjoyed the nickname.

"Because he thought she was gorgeous," Lou supplied, sure George would have a harder time admitting that.

Willow's attention, which had still been on the plants, snapped on to George. "Whoa. Okay."

"And he asked me on a date." Her shoulders pulled up toward her ears.

"Nice." Willow beamed.

But Lou frowned. "Wait. I thought you told Wesley that Austin wasn't interested in you. Did he ask you out since I saw you earlier today?"

George grinned devilishly. "Nope. He pulled me aside right after the meeting. I just didn't want Wesley to know because I didn't want him to have the satisfaction of being right about Austin being interested in me." She tapped her fingers on her lips. "Though, maybe I should've, because the way Austin was acting seemed to bother him quite a bit."

"The two of you are incorrigible." Lou clicked her tongue. "Did you find Easton?"

"We did," George confirmed. "We listed the places we're thinking of setting cameras in Button, and he helped us get permission from any businesses in the vicinity. So, we're all set for this evening."

"You have to set them up tonight?" Willow asked.

George dipped her chin, then checked her watch. "Oh, speaking of… I've got to get home to have dinner before Wesley comes back to meet me." She bolted out of her seat.

"Wait," Lou called after her. "When's your date with Austin? Where are you going? You can't just leave us hanging like this."

A bubbly laugh spilled out of George, and she said, "Right. Sorry." She plunked back down in the chair she'd just jumped out of. "He's busy this weekend, but he said he didn't want to wait until next Saturday, so we're going out Monday night. He said he wants to take me somewhere in Silver Lake, 'if I was amenable to that.'" She pushed her shoulders back. "He uses such fancy words. I'm excited."

Willow reached forward and patted George's hand with her garden-glove-clad one. "Then we're excited for you." She cut a glance outside. "Now, if you don't mind. I'm going to keep working on these smoke bushes."

"Fine. Everyone can go," Lou said with a chuckle. "George, I expect a much longer review of the date than your explanation of him asking you out."

"Fair enough." George waved over her shoulder, and then she was gone.

Lou followed Willow outside and chatted with her while she finished pruning the smoke bushes. Once she was done, Willow gave Lou a ride home, and she settled into an evening with Noah, Sapphire, and Lilli. They didn't have Marigold that evening, but it almost felt like they did with the amount of her yarn they continually found around the place—with the help of the cats, of course.

Around midnight, when Lou was just reaching the end of a chapter in the book she was reading, she got a text from Easton.

Button Up safe for tonight, it seems.

She sent back a thank-you, knowing he'd guessed she'd be up still, waiting to hear. And with that, she set her book on her bedside table, turned off her lamp, and fell into a deep sleep, snuggled up next to Noah.

THE NEXT DAY, Lou strategized with her regulars via text before the shop even opened, asking them to space out their visits. Thursdays tended to be busy, especially in the spring and summer months, and she knew she'd need their help.

Within minutes of her first message, the group had tossed around times, people had snatched up said time slots, and they'd settled upon a schedule to make sure one of them would be there to help Lou throughout the day.

George, who'd been the one to set up the group chat

between the bookshop regulars a few months prior, was likely regretting her decision after the fifty-seventh message. Based on her brief message claiming the last shift of the day, and a few seemingly annoyed thumbs-ups littered intermittently throughout the conversation, she wasn't in a great mood. Lou wondered if that was because things hadn't gone well with Wesley and the camera setup the night before. But based on the text chain, she'd have to wait until the end of the day to find out.

Lou wrote out a quick explanation of the duties she was asking of her faithful regulars, just in case another customer was in the shop when they arrived. She didn't want to give away the plan by chatting about it in front of the very person they might be trying to catch.

The book is in the gardening section. It's right next to that big green one about Pacific Northwest plants. There's a piece of paper sticking out the top, kind of like a bookmark. I need you to stay back enough that you don't scare the person away, but remember everything you can about their appearance if you notice them grabbing the piece of paper in that book.

Gloria, the first to arrive, read the information with a clipped nod and got to work. While the woman's back was slowly improving with the walking she was doing, along with some strengthening exercises to increase her core muscles, she could still only stand for a limited time. And when Gloria's strategy turned out to be lingering about, looking like she was simply searching for a book on the same aisle as any other customer, Lou knew her time would be limited. After a few breaks on the couch, and one of her favorite lattes from the café across the street, Gloria left a little early.

Lou told her it was no problem, that she could watch for the short amount of time until Forrest arrived. She only had a few customers at that time and was able to keep an eye on them under the pretense of "looking for one of the cats who liked to hide." Meanwhile, the five foster cats blinked at her conspiratorially from where they all lounged at the front of the store, and Lou hoped none of the customers looked too closely at the adoption sheets to notice that her mysterious missing cat, in fact, did not exist.

Forrest arrived after his morning appointment and was able to stay until eleven. His monitoring style was much more tranquil than Gloria's, which Lou could only describe as flustered. Forrest roamed the aisles, holding the written explanation of his duties as if it were a list of books he was searching for. This ruse allowed him to wander the aisles as needed whenever there was a customer.

He bid Lou a salute in farewell when Cricket arrived for the lunch shift, and Lou held a hand up, wishing the motion conveyed more of her gratitude.

Cricket got the verbal explanation, since she was the only customer at the time. The woman scoffed and gasped at all the appropriate moments in the tale and gave Lou a thumbs-up at the end of the explanation of her duties. She did her eagle-eyed watching mostly from the comfort of the couch, but if any customers—of which there were only two during her shift—came close to the gardening section, she made an excuse to get closer, saying she'd lost her lipstick, and swore she saw it roll under the shelf.

Silas was the only regular who employed help from the cats. Lou wasn't sure how he did it, but he and Catnip were in cahoots. Anytime he needed to follow a customer, he'd merely pretend to be chasing Catnip around. She wasn't a fan of being picked up in general, but Silas was the true love of her life, and she didn't mind him stomping around behind her, hands splayed in front of him, fingers curling and straightening in constant grabbing gestures. If he ran, she scurried ahead of him. If he stopped, so did she. This allowed him to spy on plenty of people, though none of them even ventured near the gardening section during his watch.

He left with a gruff goodbye and a tip of his signature bowler hat toward George, like ships in the night.

"Anything, so far?" George asked, settling onto a chair at the table near the front of the shop.

Lou shook her head. "The paper's still there. A few people hung out in that area, but no one touched that book."

"Why are they communicating with paper in a book?" George wrinkled her nose. "It would be so much easier to send locations and times over text or email."

"Less of a digital trail to lead back to someone?" Lou suggested.

George curled her lip. "Or the people doing the passing of messages don't know who they're dealing with." Lou could see the techie side of George's brain was having a hard time figuring out why anyone would opt against the use of technology.

A few women entered the shop. At first, Lou thought they were together, but they quickly spanned out, moving off to different sections. Lou called out a greeting to them, complimenting one on a cute, book-themed tote with a bunch of buttons stuck onto it. They each wandered through the shop but stayed far enough away from the gardening section that neither Lou nor George had to worry.

Seeing they were safe, for now, Lou returned her attention to George. "How'd everything go last night with Wesley and the cameras?" Lou asked.

George's fingers worked their way into her hair, and she tugged at it in frustration while she let out a strangled groan into the crook of her arm as if it were a sneeze.

"That well?" Lou asked with a gentle puff of a laugh.

George said something in response, but her arm muffled it.

"Come again?"

Lowering her arm away from her mouth, she fixed Lou with a guilty look and said, "I kissed Wesley."

Lou's eyes blew wide open. "What? How did that happen?"

George looked like she'd rather go sift through the shop cats' litter boxes with her bare hands than go over the details, but she croaked out a few fragments, nonetheless. "It was dark. We got close. He smelled good. I don't know! He kept doing that thing with his hair where he, like, tugs his fingers through it, and it looks all messy and sexy." She opened her hands, palms up, as if that were reason enough.

"You said *you* kissed him. What did *he* do?" Lou asked, her curiosity piqued.

George's face crumpled. "He kissed me back." She gurgled out a sound that brought to mind a dying animal. "And, of course, he's a fantastic kisser. I'm just not sure what it means," George added.

"I think it probably means ... he likes you?" Lou suggested.

But George shook her head. "Oh, no. No, no, no. That's definitely not it. The kiss was just some part of a mind game he's playing with me. The whole night, while we were setting up the cameras, he kept getting super close to me. By the time we got back to my place to confirm they were all online, he leaned in close to point something out on my computer screen. His mouth was within inches of mine. I broke down and closed the distance, but I feel like he met me halfway. It was almost as if he wanted it to happen." Her eyes narrowed. "Maybe because he knows I'm on the precipice of being happy with Austin, and he wants to get in my mind to mess that up."

"Or... And hear me out here..." Lou kept her laughter in check. "He wanted to kiss you because he wanted to kiss you, and he kept getting close so you could decide if you wanted to kiss him." George opened her lips to protest, but Lou held up a finger. "And maybe he wanted to kiss you because he likes you back, not because of some grand plan to ruin your life." She jerked her eyebrows up in question.

Now it was George's turn to hold back laughter. "Oh, Lou. You're so kind, and you think the best of everyone. No. That's definitely not it."

Lou exhaled all the hope she'd stored up. "Well, I guess

you know best." She got to her feet and went back to the new books she'd been entering into the computer for next week's new release Tuesday.

Luckily for Lou, the rest of the afternoon was rather crowded, so George was occupied for most of her shift. Her strategy seemed to be to grab a used book, plonk down on the floor next to one of the bookshelves where she could clearly see the copy of *Gulliver's Travels* but wouldn't be in the way, and pretend to read while she watched out of the corner of her eye.

And she stayed right there … until there was a giant crash outside followed by yelling.

George and Lou glanced at one another, then they raced outside into complete chaos.

One of Willow's smoke bushes was on its side, the large pot broken into a dozen pieces, potting soil strewn across the sidewalk. A man was helping another man stand up and brush off his clothes while a few other passersby craned their necks as they looked down Thread Lane, toward the roundabout in the center of town.

"What happened?" Lou asked after a moment.

"Some guy ran by and pushed him into your plant," one of the onlookers said. "It was wild. Came out of nowhere. He disappeared down the street before we could stop him."

The young man who'd been on the ground blinked, holding a hand to the back of his head. He had to be around George's age, if not a little younger.

While George assisted the people who were trying to clean up the worst of the mess and clear the sidewalk, Lou closed the distance between the injured man and herself. "Do you need me to call an ambulance? Did you hit your head?" She studied him, recognizing him enough to assume he was a local—just one she didn't speak to enough to know his name.

"No, I'm fine. Thank you." He glanced between the ruins of the pot, the mess of soil, and the bookstore. "I'm so sorry about your plant. I should pay you for the damages." He reached for the back pocket of his jeans.

Lou placed a hand on his arm, stopping him. "Thank you for the offer, but really, it's okay. The pot is replaceable. I'm just glad you're all right."

He gave her a weak smile, as if he wasn't sure that he was, but he walked off anyway.

"Lou, do you need help?" Ruby called from across the street.

Lou looked up to find the owner of the coffee shop hanging out the front door. She waved Ruby off. "I think we're okay. Thank you, though."

Ruby slipped back inside her business, and the onlookers dispersed. George came over to stand next to Lou, wiping dirt off her hands. They surveyed the damage. George and the others had managed to lean the bush against the building so its leaves wouldn't get trampled, and they'd swept as much of the soil off to the side as possible. The pot was a lost cause, but Lou would have to get Willow's opinion on what needed to be done for the poor plant.

Now that the worst of the commotion was over, Lou and George glanced back at the bookshop, which they'd left unattended. Gasping in unison, they raced back inside. The three women who'd been shopping were all gone.

Sprinting for the copy of *Gulliver's Travels*, Lou's taut

shoulders loosened in relief when she caught sight of the paper still sticking out from the center.

"Phew," said George, sinking against the bookshelf. "I thought for sure that was a distraction created by the thieves, just like the kitten."

Lou had to agree, as did the uneasy feeling in her gut. And even though the paper remained, she had a bad feeling they'd just been duped.

CHAPTER 11

Lou's fears were confirmed that Friday night at eleven when she got a text from Easton.

She dropped the book she'd been reading in bed. Noah looked over from the one he was reading, setting his down with more care than she had.

"They hit the outdoor shop," she explained breathlessly as she typed out a response to Easton.

She wished he wasn't being so cryptic. He had to know what questions she would ask after learning that information. Taking a moment to think compassionately, she figured it had just happened, and he was trying to do his job at the same time as keeping her informed.

His response came through a moment later.

We did not. They came early. They were
long gone by the time we got here.

She suddenly understood the reason behind Easton's vague texts. He must be frustrated they hadn't been able to stop it from happening, even though Easton had been right about the day.

Noah, who'd been waiting patiently, laid a hand over Lou's, reminding her she still needed to fill him in.

Her gaze drifted up to his, softening in silent apology. "They were gone by the time Easton and the police arrived at ten."

"They knew the police were aware of the time," he summarized.

"But they never took the paper." Lou swallowed thickly as she thought about the implications. "They must've figured out that we'd seen the paper and were setting them up, so they set us up instead." Frustration warred with anger in her heart.

Noah threaded his fingers through hers, as if sensing that she needed some grounding. "Look at it this way. At least no one was hurt."

She loved him for his attempts to get her to stop blaming herself. "I'm just mad that they slipped through our fingers twice."

"Twice?" Noah asked.

"Tonight, with the police, and yesterday at the book-shop. Remember when I told you about that guy being pushed into one of the smoke bushes in front of the shop?"

Noah nodded. He'd offered to come help clean up, but

Willow had the thing repotted and cleaned up before Lou had even closed for the day.

"Well, I think that was a distraction they created to get me and George out of the shop so they could check the note. But instead of taking it, they must've read the code and put it back to fool us." She kneaded her fingers into her temple. "There's another silver lining, actually. We know when they came in to look at the paper." She wrinkled her nose as something else became clear now that she knew it was all a farce. "And now I'm realizing that the young man who knocked the plant over was one of the two who pulled the first job with the kitten. That's why I recognized him—not because he was a local."

While she talked, Lou brought up the security app on her phone and toggled to that time of the day. She and Noah scooted closer as the footage from that time period played on.

Lou held her breath as she watched herself and George dash out the shop door. Things were steady for a moment as two of the women who'd been inside followed her and George outside to help. But then, movement toward the gardening aisle caught Lou's eye.

"There," she said, pointing at the screen. Her finger accidentally poked the video, causing it to pause just as the third woman stopped in front of the copy of *Gulliver's Travels*.

She was probably about Lou's age and had shoulder-length, curly brown hair, which she kept swept in front of her face anytime she had to turn even remotely toward the camera. Lou immediately remembered her. She'd complimented the woman on her bag, which had a cute saying about books printed on the side. What had it said? *It's a good day to read a book*? Yes, that was it. And there were cute pins clipped all over it as well.

Other than her bag, however, Lou couldn't remember anything else of interest about the woman. She squinted at the screen, hoping to remember something else that could identify her.

Hitting the screen again, she let the video resume. The woman paused near the book and then turned to leave.

"You saw her take it off the shelf, right?" Lou asked, moving the phone even closer.

"If I'm being honest, I can't see anything on that tiny display." Noah chuckled. "What do you say we try this on a bigger screen?"

They climbed out of bed, padding into the living room and hooking the phone up to the television screen. Once the phone was plugged in, the image showed much larger.

"Better," Noah said.

Lou pressed play on the phone, and the video continued on the television. Lou backed it up a few seconds so they could see the full event.

The woman with the cute bag stopped, pulled out the book, flipped to the page the piece of paper had book-marked, read over the paper for a few seconds while she put together the code, then she shut the book and slid it back onto the shelf. The whole thing was over in a minute.

Lou was about to pause the video there when Noah jabbed a finger at the screen. "Did you see that?"

Shaking her head, Lou backed up the video to the moment where the woman put the book back. Something outside the store startled her, quickening her movements, and she spun on her heel, bolting out of the aisle. But in the process, her bag caught on the corner of the shelf, snagged for a moment, and something fell to the floor. The item on the floor disappeared underneath the bookshelf as the woman raced out the front door.

"There were a bunch of buttons on the exterior of the bag. One of them must've snagged," Lou said.

"Maybe it could help identify her, since she kept her face turned away from the camera the whole time."

"Maybe," Lou answered, wistfully. She wasn't sure how a pin might help them, but it was worth a shot.

Unplugging the phone from the television, Lou promised to search for the pin tomorrow. She would also ask George how to isolate that video file so she could send it to Easton.

Lou fell asleep hard after that, but her dreams were filled with nightmares of thieves sneaking into her most treasured spaces, making her safe havens feel unstable.

THE NEXT MORNING, Lou checked under the bookshelf for the pin.

There wasn't anything there.

Lou couldn't spend more time searching than that, however, because it was Saturday, her busiest day of the week. That day was no exception, especially since it was sunny and gorgeous out, making for a crowded downtown filled with smiling, happy tourists.

With George's help, Lou isolated the video file for Easton after work. It was a lengthier process than she'd expected, but George explained that it was mostly due to half the officers being technologically behind the times, so she defaulted to something they could all use, like a USB drive.

"Easton's better than most," George explained with a chuckle. "But he still gets confused if I start talking about cloud sharing."

Lou thanked her for her help and pocketed the drive so she could pass it off to Easton.

After that, Lou didn't have a moment to think about the pin again. The town held a celebration of life for Heather that Sunday morning and the emotions of it all, as well as the terrible closure of saying goodbye, overtook Lou's mind until she was back at the bookshop later that day.

A scraping sound caught Lou's attention during one of her slower periods in the afternoon. It was intermittent and sounded like someone was rolling a marble across the bookshop's wood floors. Upon investigation, Lou found Mr. Clawrcy batting something small and metal around in the nonfiction section. The object had a flat face with a sharp pin sticking out of the back. Lou knelt next to the large cat.

He reared back at her sudden movement.

"Sorry, Clawrcy," she cooed at the cat, holding her hand out toward him in a slower motion that earned back his trust. He sniffed her hand before rubbing his head against it, the affront forgiven.

Lou slowly shifted her hand from the cat to the item on the floor. It was a pin, but not one of the snarky ones with dumpster fires or raccoons claiming to love trash that had caught her eye on the bag. It looked like some kind of coat of arms, with a badger in the center, and blue and silver accents.

Knowing she might very well regret it, Lou took a picture and added it to the group chat between her and the shop regulars.

> Does anyone recognize this logo?

George answered almost immediately.

> That's the crest for Silver Lake High School. I remember seeing it whenever our sports teams had to play theirs.

While it wasn't out of the question that Lou could've gotten the woman's age wrong from the video footage, she felt confident in saying she had not been young enough to go to high school. Was she the parent of a high schooler? A teacher?

Sending back a thank-you text, Lou was glad George had cleared that up so quickly. She probably hadn't needed to ask the whole group.

To add further insult to injury, the rest of the regulars didn't seem to think George's confirmation was enough. They each chimed in with their own messages that it definitely looked like the Silver Lake High School logo. Well, all except Gloria, who felt the need to write three messages explaining how she didn't recognize it and then explaining that she didn't pay attention to what happened in Silver Lake since they were all stuck-up snobs.

Lou couldn't help but giggle at the antics of the group. Separately, she sent George a text.

Sorry. I should've asked you first. You're going to leave the group now, aren't you?

George sent back an eye-rolling emoji.

I should. I would if I didn't love them all so much.

That settled, Lou finished out the day, excited to share the news about the pin with Easton and Noah.

She pulled up to the house just before six that evening. She stopped to grab the mail, parking back far enough that she had to walk past the Little Free Library she'd installed last year, when Easton had still been living here. It was a habit to look inside whenever she passed it, wondering what books were gone and which had taken their place. She smiled as she noticed a few of the newer books she'd put inside were gone, swapped with older, well-loved paperbacks. Lou didn't care how many books cycled through the tiny library. She got a thrill out of the exchange each time.

Once she got back in the car and drove the rest of the way up the driveway, Lou found Noah and Easton working in the garden together while Marigold raced around with Steve on her heels and Willow exercised OC in the arena.

Lou wandered over to them, leaning into Noah as he brought his arm around her shoulders and greeted her with a kiss.

"I found the pin," she told him.

Noah's brow constricted, but it was Easton who asked, "The one from the smoke-bush distraction?"

"Yes." She produced it from her bag. "It's from Silver Lake High School."

"She has to be a parent or a teacher, then," Noah said.

"That's what I'm thinking," Lou agreed.

Easton twisted a large dandelion from the ground, running the back of his hand over his cheek to catch a drop of sweat. "Great. There aren't a ton of teachers and parents who might fit the description of a middle-aged white woman who might be connected to the school." Sarcasm dripped from the statement. "I guess I'll have to look into that on Monday when I'm out there for my meeting with the Silver Lake detectives—*if* the meeting doesn't take all day, which it probably will since Detective Lorens loves to hear himself talk."

Lou caught Noah's eye before saying, "We could always go, if you want."

Easton tossed the dandelion into the open yard waste bin. "Really?"

"Absolutely," Noah said. "Plus, if they're already changing things up because they think we're onto them, it might be better for us to be asking around about this woman instead of a cop."

Easton huffed out a grateful sigh. "That would be great. I'll talk to the Silver Lake detectives about it on Monday as well, but if you two would do a preliminary check to see if you can narrow it down, I'd really appreciate it."

That settled, Lou jogged inside to change into some gardening friendly clothes so she could help them. While she was inside, an email came through from the Whiskers and Words website. The subject line read, **Gullipurr Sighting**. Inside, a local had attached a picture of Gullipurr walking along someone's fence. His orange face was pointed up to the sky, probably watching a bird, but Lou already had the perfect caption to add to that tomorrow at work. *Gullipurr searches the sky for the floating city of Laputa.*

She smiled to herself as she sent a thank-you email back to the sender. Between this and the lead in their case, Gullipurr wasn't the only thing looking up.

CHAPTER 12

Lou closed the bookstore at lunch on Monday, waiting for Noah while he finished up his last appointment for the day. Then they drove to Silver Lake, making sure to arrive about twenty minutes after school had let out for the day. The high school was housed in a formidable building.

"It looks a bit like a prison, if I'm being honest," Lou said as she stared up at it.

"Lady, you have no idea," mumbled a teenage boy as he walked by them in the parking lot.

She and Noah exchanged amused grins before going inside. The sharp corners of the pin dug into Lou's palm as she clutched it.

Inside, instead of the expected aromas of a high school, they were met with an overwhelming wall of men's cologne, as if one of the teenagers had gone too far in trying to cover up his body odor.

"I feel like I just stepped inside a can of Axe body spray." Lou flinched, blinking as the smell reached her eyes.

Noah laughed, but it turned into a cough. "Teenage armpits would actually be preferable to this."

A janitor rushed by, propping open the doors Noah and Lou had just walked through as she wafted a rag in front of her face. "Sorry. Some kids were tossing around a bottle of cologne after school, and it spilled all over the hall. We're still trying to air everything out."

"No problem," Noah said, pointing down the hall. "Main office?"

The janitor jerked her head in a nod. "Yep. Straight ahead. Can't miss it."

Lou resisted the urge to pull her T-shirt up over her nose to filter out the worst of the smell.

"I think we're walking toward the site of the incident," Noah said, his voice tight as his lungs attempted to pull in as little air as possible.

Just when the cologne smell became almost unbearable, a large sign signaled that they'd reached the office. But the moment they stepped inside, the aroma became three times worse. Despite every window in the place being open wide, the air was thick with the musky, spiced cologne. The fact that about ten teenage boys were also crowded in the chairs lining the edge of the room didn't seem to be a coincidence.

The boys had no qualms about using their T-shirts as masks, and each looked like a turtle, the bottom half of their faces tucked inside. From within their shirts, periodic giggles escaped the boys as they shot one another conspiratorial glances and threw elbows at each other.

An exasperated blonde woman, who also looked like she might be on the verge of passing out, based on the reddish tint to her cheeks, glanced up as Lou and Noah entered.

"I'm sorry. We're dealing with a bit of a crisis at the moment. I'll be just one minute." Her sentences were rushed, as if she were trying not to breathe in. The second she finished speaking, she pivoted toward the open window and sucked in a breath of the fresh air.

"Do you mind if we wait in the hall?" Lou asked, jerking her thumb back toward the way they'd come.

"No problem," the woman said, understanding coating her statement. "I'll come get you once we take care of this lot." She glowered at the gaggle of boys, prompting another round of nervous laughter and coughing to erupt from them.

Noah held the door. Lou held her breath. They both dragged air into their lungs the moment they stepped into the hallway.

"I think that poor woman's going to be asphyxiated if she doesn't get out of there soon." Noah chuckled.

Lou leaned back against a row of lockers, painted blue to match the Silver Lake school colors. She closed her eyes and inhaled. "I'm guessing those were our cologne throwers." When Noah didn't answer, she blinked her eyes open once more.

Noah wasn't listening. A dimpled grin took over his expression, and he moved forward. "Sorry, but I was just remembering another case we worked together. The one where we did this for the first time." He placed his hands on either side of Lou's head, leaning down to capture her lips in a kiss.

She kissed him back before moving to the side to make

sure no one was in the hall with them. "I feel like I'm back in high school and we're not supposed to be showing public displays of affection in the hallway." A giggle escaped her, proving she probably belonged with the boys in the office.

But Noah only moved closer. "Was high school Louisa a rule follower?" he asked in between kisses.

Nodding, Lou said, "Terribly so."

He pulled back, eyes shining with interest. "I want to hear all about her." When Lou shook her head, Noah countered by saying, "Hey, you got to see my embarrassing high school yearbook photos."

Lou tsked. "Ah, yes. It's incredibly embarrassing that you were the homecoming king and popular. High school Lou would've loved you from afar, while hiding in the library, where she spent most of her time."

Noah's lips curved into a dashing smile. "High school Noah had a soft spot for girls who read all the time. He would've found high school Lou incredibly attractive." Another kiss, this one longer. "Still does."

A woman cleared her throat behind them.

Lou couldn't back up any farther because of the lockers, so she sank down a few inches while Noah whirled around. The woman from the main office stood there, hip cocked. She wore an unamused expression as plainly as her purple cardigan.

"Can I help you?" she asked, not even needing to tap her toe on the floor; impatience poured off her without the motion.

"Yes, I own a shop in Button, and someone dropped this the other day." Lou stepped forward, holding the pin in her palm so the woman could get a good look. "I'm wondering if you could tell me what it is."

Mrs. Highgate, as Lou read off the name tag pinned to her sweater, lifted her chin and studied the pin. "Oh, that's one of our honor society pins. A student must've dropped that."

"That's the thing," Lou said with a frown. "The woman who I think lost this was my age."

Mrs. Highgate narrowed her eyes. "Can I see that again?"

Lou held it out again. That time, Mrs. Highgate took the pin.

"Oh, sorry. I didn't see the star on the bottom. That's a special one that we give out to our teachers who have a certain percentage of their class in honor society." She gave Lou a suspicious once-over. "But we give them out for free, so it's not like the person won't get another one if they want. You really didn't have to go through the trouble of returning it." Still, she tucked it into her cardigan pocket.

"Right," Lou said, moving her palm up to slap against her forehead. "Sure. I just thought... I don't know why I thought it might be important. Sorry to bother you." She glanced over her shoulder at Noah, signaling it was time to go.

They began walking, opting for the set of exterior doors they could see, rather than walking through the long hallway they'd come through. Lou appreciated the decision, more than willing to walk around the exterior of the building to get back to the car rather than braving more time within the stinky halls.

But before they reached the double doors nearest to

them, Lou stopped next to a display case near the entrance. Inside hung pictures of the staff members.

"If she's a teacher, the woman we're looking for should be here," she said as her eyes pored over each photograph. "We might not know what her face looks like, but we know she has brown hair that's on the curly side. About shoulder length."

There were three such women who fit that description. Mrs. Cowell from the English department, Miss Heller, a creative writing teacher, and Miss Klegg, the drama teacher. Lou took quick pictures of each one of them to share with Easton, and then they left.

"Well, all three of them seem likely to own a cute reading tote. I think Easton can take it from here. I'll be happy if I never have to go back there," she muttered. "I don't think I'll ever get the scent of that cologne out of my nose."

"I think it might've seeped into my skin." Noah pulled the collar of his shirt up to his nose. "Here, check my shirt. Do I smell like it?"

Lou turned toward Noah and leaned forward to sniff. The moment she was close enough, Noah placed a kiss on her forehead, then tilted her chin up to plant a kiss on her lips.

A happy heat moved into her cheeks at the fact that she'd fallen for that. "I think high school Noah was a flirt."

"He never grew up." Noah wrapped an arm around her, and they walked to the car. When they arrived, he said, "What if we did something to make this trip less of a bust?"

Lou cocked her head. "I'm game."

"I hear the walking path around Silver Lake is beautiful,

and it's about four miles long." Checking his watch, he said, "So if we do that, it might be around dinnertime by the time we finish, and there's a Thai restaurant I've heard is pretty good."

"Sounds perfect." Lou climbed into the car.

After a gorgeous and relaxing walk along the water—during which they finally got the smell of cologne from their noses and had to admit that Silver Lake was quite beautiful—they headed for the restaurant. They'd both worked up quite an appetite.

Their server had just left with their orders when George walked through the front door of the restaurant. Surprise filled Lou, but spiked as she noticed Austin accompanied her. That was right. George's date with Austin had been Monday night in Silver Lake. She waved them over.

"Hey," George said, a big smile on her face. "What are you two doing?"

"Just salvaging a failed outing," Noah said.

"To do with the case?" George asked.

Lou turned to Austin to explain. "Some of my stolen books have been returned with odd notes inside them. We're just trying to figure out why."

Questions wrote themselves across Austin's face, but Lou waved a hand to dismiss them. He and George obviously had more important things to think about than hearing about high school pins and bad cologne.

"Sorry," Lou added. "You're on a date. We won't keep you."

There was a hesitation in George's body language as she stepped back from the table. Austin, watching her closely, seemed to catch her stalling.

"Or, if you want, and your friends don't mind, we could join them." He placed a hand on George's arm.

"You'd be more than welcome to," Noah said, motioning to the two open seats at their table.

George's eyes lit up, but she quickly schooled her expression. "I wouldn't want to do that on our first date."

"Nonsense. We can always have dinner by ourselves on our next date." Austin chuckled nervously, his cheeks reddening. "Sorry if that's forward of me to assume we'll have another date."

There was a brightness in George's eyes as she said, "Don't apologize. I like the confidence." She took a seat next to Lou while Austin slid into the spot next to Noah. "I was once on a date where we'd both decided within the first few minutes that we wouldn't work, so this is already so much better."

"With Wesley, right?" Austin asked.

George had obviously forgotten they'd told him that story at the chamber of commerce meeting, because her cheeks reddened with embarrassment.

Austin scoffed. "I can't imagine someone deciding they don't want to see you again."

Lou and Noah exchanged a quick grin. George practically beamed.

Austin scratched the back of his neck. "Honestly, I was surprised when you said yes. I thought there might be something going on with you and Wesley."

George took a gulp of air in her surprise, but caught herself, turning it into a cough. "Me and Wesley? No. No way." She shook her head and cut the air with her hand, as if only one negative gesture wasn't enough.

The server saved her from adding anything else to the pile of objections, coming to take George and Austin's orders so their food would come out with Noah's and Lou's. From there, they segued into talking about how each of the bookshop owners at the table had come to own their respective businesses.

Lou told her story, and then listened as Austin explained how Rupert, the former owner of Silver Lake Books, mentioned he was looking to sell during one of Austin's almost weekly visits to the store. Austin, who'd been saving for a house, couldn't pass up the opportunity, especially since the shop had an apartment above like Lou's. So, he'd invested in the business instead.

"And here I am," he said. "I couldn't be happier. Though, I think you've got the right idea with all your cats. I might need to add a few to my shop as well. I've been wanting one forever, but I could never have animals in any of the places I rented."

George sent him an equally radiant look back, and Lou's heart warmed. It was good to see George happy.

"Have you always loved books, then?" Lou asked as their food arrived, and they all began to dig in.

Austin nodded. "I've always loved the written word, but I really got into it when my grandfather passed and left me a bunch of his journals and writing paraphernalia." He let out a reminiscent chuckle. "The man thought he was going to be the next Hemingway."

"Do you write too?" Noah asked.

Scoffing, Austin said, "No, no. I'm content to read the brilliant words of others. I definitely don't have what it takes to be a published author."

George laid a hand on his arm. "Same. I don't even read all that much," she admitted, twisting her mouth into a grimace. "Unless you count D and D, and all the reading I do while gaming."

"We do." Lou fixed her with a pointed look, having tried to convince her that reading could look different from the narrow definition George had grown up with.

"I'm okay if you don't consider yourself a reader, you know," Austin chimed in. "I'm into the whole opposites-attract idea." At that, he sent her a bright smile that seemed to make George melt.

Lou and Noah each used that moment to take a big bite of their dinners, grinning at one another from across the table.

CHAPTER 13

The next day, Lou woke to a text from Easton.

When you get to the bookshop today, would you check if there's another book?

Her stomach sank.

Was there another break-in?

Unfortunately, yes. The florist in Brine this time.

Easton, I'm so sorry. I didn't see any books yesterday, but I closed early so I didn't have time to look before Noah and I took off for Silver Lake.

I didn't mean to make you feel bad. You
closed early so you could help me out.
Thank you, by the way. I already have a
team researching the three teachers you
sent over info on. I was just asking about
the book because I'm wondering if they're
changing their information system now
that they know we're onto them. Purely
research.

She told him she'd check first thing when she got to the shop that day. Despite using all the time she had after feeding the cats and doing her opening chores, Lou couldn't find the book. Luckily, all Lou's regulars showed up first thing that morning, and they got to work searching when she told them about the text from Easton.

She was starting to think he was right, that maybe the thieves had changed their MO, when Gloria found what they were looking for shelved with the cookbooks.

"Is there a note inside?" Lou asked.

Gloria flipped through the pages, but nothing came fluttering out.

"So, they only left the one in the other day because… Why? They knew we were watching them?" Lou worried her bottom lip as she thought through the implications of this new piece of information.

Her regulars chattered about what they thought while Lou texted Easton about what they'd found.

"I bet that woman just forgot to take the paper that last time," Gloria said. "I forget stuff all the time, and it's definitely not strategic." She snorted out a laugh.

Cricket tilted her head in agreement. "Fair point."

"It's interesting because the thieves simultaneously

present themselves as amateurs when they do things like use kittens to distract their victims and leave notes behind, but it could just as easily be a deep, long-term strategy." Forrest, ever the contemplative thinker, ran his fingers along his jawline as he considered it all.

Silas snorted. "I agree with Forrest." When everyone looked at him in surprise, he said, "This is all some big plan. None of it is by accident. Well, maybe none of it except Heather's death." He dipped his chin for a moment in silence before adding, "The strategy is Lou." He poked a stubby finger at her.

"Me?" Lou placed a hand on her chest.

"You." Silas nodded. "You're the first one they hit. Your shop is where they're dropping their little hints to one another. You're the common denominator."

Cricket guffawed. "Oh, come off it, Silas. Lou just happened to be the first victim."

Gloria, George, and even Forrest reluctantly agreed with Cricket.

The speculation continued—and grew wilder still—until the group departed a short while later. Well, almost the entire group. When Lou glanced around the shop, she noticed George had hung back. The young woman sat on the floor in a puddle of oversized basketball shorts and a large T-shirt with a dragon on it, surrounded by cats.

And even though that was a normal position for her friend, Lou could tell something was up. She'd yet to have any customers other than her regulars just yet, so Lou got down on the floor, crisscrossed her legs, and studied George.

"You and Austin seemed to hit it off last night." Lou

scratched Jane Pawsten's ears when the cat trotted over to her.

George pressed her lips together. She wouldn't quite meet Lou's gaze, her eyes flicking back down to the floor if they strayed up to her face.

"But you're not feeling him?" Lou guessed.

That earned her George's focus. "That's not it," she protested, eyes wide and earnest. "I like Austin a lot, and I think he's good for me." She scooted closer to Lou. "He says exactly what he's thinking all the time. I don't have to wonder how he feels about me because he tells me."

Lou had noticed the same during dinner as well—a pleasant surprise and something George had liked, if the moony-eyed stares she sent his way during their meal were anything to go by.

A chuckle burst out of Lou. "George, those are all good things. You've gotta help me out here. If he's so great, why do you look miserable?"

"Because even though he's everything I've been hoping for, I have an appointment to go through surveillance footage with Wesley tonight, and I can't stop thinking about the last time when we kissed." She covered her face with her hands.

Sensing her anguish, the cats flocked to George, all rubbing against her or attempting to climb into her lap. It was just the kind of levity the situation called for, and Lou grew even more in love with each of her foster felines.

"Are you sure Austin is everything you want?" Lou asked tentatively. The two had appeared compatible at dinner, but Lou knew love was often so much more than compatibility—sometimes even the complete opposite.

George looked up, a divot forming in between her eyebrows.

Seeing she needed to clarify, Lou added, "Your feelings for Wesley have … endured. I know Willow's not here, but I can say for certain that both she and I tried to fight against what we felt for Easton and Noah, respectively. She did it by convincing herself that he hated her, and I used a bit of confirmation bias to prove to myself that Noah wasn't ready to move on from his divorce."

"Maybe." George sighed. "But if he felt the same about me, why hasn't he told me or… I mean, I don't mind being the one to make the first move. I need him to at least give me some sign that he feels the same. But even after I kissed him, it's been awkward silence ever since." Shrugging, George added, "No, I owe it to myself to see where things go with Austin. And that's why I really need your help tonight."

"Okay." Lou studied her friend.

"I need you to tag along tonight when I have to work with Wesley." George's expression was deadpan.

"What? I—That's—I can't—" Lou pushed up off the floor, feeling the need to pace. "How will we explain that?"

"Easy," George scoffed. "You're invested in the case. You've been investigating into things, too, and you'd like to look at the footage to see if anything sticks out to you."

Contemplating that for a moment, Lou had to admit it wasn't the worst excuse. Finally, she said, "I guess I could pretend to be nosy and need to tag along."

A small snort escaped George. "Sure. Pretend." She stifled a laugh as she got to her feet. "Thanks, Lou. I'll text you the time and place we're going to meet. Though, I'm going to push for Wesley's place since we met at mine last time, and we know how that ended. I'm sure his is a crusty bachelor pad, which will only help me quash anything from happening."

With that, George left. Lou spent the rest of the morning practicing for her babysitting job that evening. Well, that's what it felt like as she followed her customers around, watching them like a hawk to make sure they weren't bringing a book in with them or placing it on a shelf. If the every-three-days pattern was to continue, another would show up in the next twenty-four hours or so, and Lou was determined to catch them.

By lunchtime, she still hadn't. Frustrated, Lou ran her sales numbers for the week, checking to see if she could call it quits early, as she often did on her slower days.

Also, if I'm closed, they can't plant a book here, her subconscious argued. But that argument plummeted through the floor as she found she hadn't sold a single book yet that week.

Right. Between closing early yesterday and all but chasing customers away with her lurking today, what more could she expect? Deflated, Lou closed early anyway. She sulked across the street, bought two sandwiches from Ruby at the café, and took them to Noah's clinic down the road.

"Hi, doll," Kathleen, the clinic manager, greeted Lou as she entered the waiting room.

A cat screeched out its objections at being there, from within a small crate, and a large German shepherd sat on the other side of the room. It stared at the sandwiches in Lou's hands with an intense focus.

"Hi, Kathleen." Lou smiled in greeting. "Noah in the back?"

Kathleen jerked her head to the side with a wink, showing her she could go through. Lou thanked her and skirted around the reception desk and into the treatment space behind the patient rooms. Noah's office was next to the surgery room, and he sat behind his computer.

When she knocked on the door, his expression morphed out of the concentrated scowl it had been in and turned into something so bright that Lou almost wanted to cry.

"Everything okay?" His attention caught on the sandwiches, and he looked even more confused.

"It's fine." Lou sank into the chair in the corner of his office. "I closed the bookshop early and brought you lunch."

Noah's gaze flicked to the clock hanging on his wall, proving he'd lost track of time and hadn't even realized it was lunch. "You're amazing. I just have to get Cheese her prescription and then do an exam on Suki, and then I have a break."

"Cheese is … the cat? And Suki's the German shepherd?" Lou guessed.

"Other way around, actually." Noah checked one more thing on the screen, clicked a few buttons, and then stood. "Start without me if you're hungry." Noah kissed the top of her head before he walked out the door.

She waited, setting them up in the staff lunchroom, but was contemplating taking him up on his offer to eat, when Noah walked through the door.

"Everything okay with Suki?" Lou asked conversationally.

"Great, actually. She had some bladder stones, and we were considering surgery, but the X-rays show they've completely dissolved with the prescription diet we've had her on. So, great news." He grabbed them both sparkling waters from the fridge before joining Lou at the table. Instead of picking up his sandwich, he asked, "And you closed early today because...?"

It wasn't unusual for Lou to take a half day on Monday and Tuesday—sometimes even closing altogether—which meant that her body language must've given away that something was wrong.

"I'm paranoid. I spent the morning following customers around and asking them prying questions. It's no wonder no one felt comfortable to stay long enough to buy a book." Puffing out her cheeks, she took a bite of her sandwich. "So, I'm going to go home after this and go for a nice long run instead. Oh, and if we don't have any other plans, I'm going with George to Wesley's tonight to look through some surveillance footage."

One of Noah's eyebrows twitched.

"She needs backup," she said with a smirk.

Noah mirrored her expression but didn't push the issue. "No problem. Easton and I are going to start prep for that bigger turnout field for OC that we were discussing the other night."

They moved on to more pleasant subjects after that. And by the time Lou left to go home to change for her run, she already felt miles better.

"Good luck babysitting tonight," Noah called after Lou as she left.

I'm gonna need it, she thought.

CHAPTER 14

Wesley lived in possibly the only modern-looking home in the town of Brine. While every other structure was made of old brick or featured intricate, craftsman-style details, Wesley's house was sleek, rectangular, and full of windows. Lou, who was not usually a fan of modern design, actually liked the look of the place from the outside. She shared George's worry about the state of the interior, however.

That made it even more surprising when he opened the door and a whoosh of cinnamon- and sugar-scented air wafted out toward them. Also surprising—Wesley didn't even appear mildly caught off guard to see her.

"Hey, Lou." Wesley tucked his chin in greeting, his sandy-blond hair falling forward with the movement. "George."

His laid-back attitude made questions crop up in Lou's mind. "Did George warn you I was coming this evening?"

He and George shook their heads in tandem.

"I guess I was just surprised it took you this long to get

involved in the surveillance part of it all, honestly." He stepped back so they could enter.

"See?" George whispered to Lou under her breath as they stepped inside.

But Lou couldn't focus on her frustration with her friend because something else caught her attention—a rather elderly tuxedo cat tottering over to the front door from wherever it had been sleeping, if its mussed fur, flattened on one side, was any indication.

Wesley's cheeks turned a little red as he closed the door and glanced around them to see what had caught their attention. "Ah, meet Fig."

"Fig?" George breathed out the name, looking like someone had just slapped her across the face.

And Lou knew exactly why. She, too, was replaying the conversations they'd had that past February about how Wesley couldn't take Mr. Clawrcy when he'd found him wandering behind a warehouse in Kirk. Lou—and George, by extension—had assumed it was because Wesley wasn't a cat person. It was a fact that had become a sort of line drawn in the sand for George since her cat, Geralt, was a huge part of her life.

But living evidence refuting that claim toddled over to them, blinking as it meowed in greeting. Looking up, however, proved too challenging for its balance, and the poor thing almost toppled over. Wesley uttered a little "Oops" before bending to scoop the cat into his arms.

Fig immediately began purring up a storm. The cat gazed lovingly at Wesley for a moment before leaning in to rub against his chin. He laughed affectionately. "Don't worry, girl. I've got you."

George looked downright catatonic.

"Earlier this year … you couldn't take Mr. Clawrcy because of Fig," Lou said, needing to get the thoughts out of her mind.

"Yeah," he said, sheepishly. "Figgy's almost twenty, and she's never been fond of other cats. Bringing another cat, especially one who was as cranky as Clawrcy was at first, didn't seem like a good idea. I just want to give her a quiet, happy life as long as I can. She's been my cat since I was five."

Lou stepped forward, running a gentle hand over Fig's soft head. Wesley grinned, stepping around them so he could lead them farther into the house, something Lou wasn't sure George was capable of at first. She resisted the urge to snap her fingers in front of her friend's face. Finally, George escaped her trance, and she followed as they moved beyond the entryway.

The interior was also quite the surprise, though Lou wasn't sure anything could top Fig. Wesley's home was just that: a home. It was decorated. It had a cohesive, cozy style. A smart tweed couch sat in the center of a clean living room with a coffee table and a tastefully sized television.

In fact, of the two twenty-year-olds in the room, George's house was more of what Lou might've expected from a bachelor.

As if he could hear the questions screaming through the minds of the two women in his home, Wesley said, "Sebastian technically owns the place, but he's letting me rent to own." His cheeks colored as he mentioned his rich client, a mutual friend of theirs, as if Lou hadn't already been wondering how he was able to afford the place. "He knew the old owner and got a good deal because he gave him cash."

"That's very nice of him," Lou said, though she wasn't surprised in the least. Sebastian Andrade had proven himself to be a genuinely kind and benevolent person. He also had a soft spot for Wesley St. James, beyond the private investigation work the young man often did for him.

"And I can't claim the decorations either. This is all Bea from The Upholstered Button. I took my first big paycheck after a private investigation job to her and asked her to go wild." He scanned the space fondly.

George's mouth tightened into a hard line as she looked around.

"Well, Bea did a great job. It's a beautiful home, Wesley." Lou wasn't sure if she was covering for the young woman's silence or trying to make up for her sour attitude. Maybe it was both.

Wesley dipped his head in thanks.

Obviously less impressed, George asked, "Where are we going to look through the surveillance files?" She put her hand on her hip.

A smug smirk pulled across Wesley's lips as George threw her mini-fit. Stepping to the first door in the hallway next to the living room, Wesley opened the door and asked, "Will this do?"

Inside what was probably meant to be a bedroom, Wesley had created a home office that put anything Lou had ever seen to shame. Like the living room, it was also smartly decorated with a large wooden desk, a full wall of bookshelves, and a leather office chair. The picture window along the biggest wall overlooked the meadow behind Wesley's home.

"Oh." George's lips parted, and she stepped inside so she could take it all in.

She sank into what Lou was sure was a very expensive office chair and ran her fingertips over the keyboard and track pad on the desk.

Lou's attention shifted to Wesley, whose expression had wholly morphed the moment George sat down. His smirk had disappeared, replaced by a reverent, hopeful kind of look. Lou's heart ached watching the two of them in this dance of miscommunication. She also felt incredibly uncomfortable, as if she definitely shouldn't be there.

Most of the time, Lou didn't feel the age gap between herself and George. At that moment, however, she felt ancient. She felt like she was a school dance chaperone whom the young kids might roll their eyes at when she started waxing poetic about the "music from back in my day."

"Okay, where do we start?" Lou asked, hoping to chase away the awkward feelings.

Wesley brought in two chairs from his dining table— yes, because he was a young man with a dining table—and set them up around the computer. The screen was curved and so wide they were all able to see without anyone having to lean in close at all. So, it seemed George had been right about Wesley's house being better for keeping her distance … just not for the reasons she'd expected.

He let George sit in the middle, in the nicest chair, arguing that she'd be the one driving most of the navigation. To prove her competence, George logged on to the app where the surveillance files were sent and entered her passwords.

"Look away," she deadpanned. "I wouldn't want anyone but me to know these passwords."

Lou bit back a giggle.

Once George was logged in, Wesley said, "I think the camera we placed on Cornichon Street will be our best bet if it was the florist that was hit."

"We're looking at Monday night, right?" George asked Lou.

Lou had to school her expression after hearing the silly, pickle-themed name of the street. "Yes." Her lips twitched into the beginnings of a smile, so she pursed them for a moment to regain control. "But we didn't get the paper for that one, so all we know is that it happened sometime between when they closed for the day and when they went to open in the morning."

George pulled up the footage, and Lou found herself watching the parking lot and front entrance to the florist in Brine. A pair of employees locked up and left, driving off in the remaining two cars in the parking lot.

They'd already gone through a few hours of footage when Lou gasped. "Stop the video there."

"Why?" George asked. "There are no people on the screen yet."

Lou's finger shot out to show where a large orange cat limped across the parking lot. "Is that Gullipurr?"

"Who?" Wesley snorted.

"A cat that roams all over Button," George scoffed, as if it was common knowledge. "Lou calls him Gullipurr because of his travels. She's got the whole town following his movements and relating them back to the Johnathan Swift novel."

Quick as lightning, George opened a second browser, pulled up the Whiskers and Words site, and showed Wesley Lou's *Gullipurr's Travels* blog.

"You made a whole blog dedicated to Hissie?" Wesley leaned closer to get a better look.

"Hissie?" George and Lou asked at the same time.

Wesley inclined his head. "He's been a stray in Brine for years. Well, for the first year, only a handful of people believed he existed, and the people who swore they'd seen him didn't have proof. The locals started calling him Hissie."

"Like Nessie." George blew a laugh from her nose.

"That, and he hisses at anyone who gets close. We've since gathered many sightings, as well as pictures, of the big guy. No one's ever been able to catch him." Wesley shrugged.

Lou's stomach flipped with unease. "That's concerning because it looks like he's hurt."

Sensing Lou needed proof, George clicked on the video again and it played. Unlike the other times Lou had encountered the cat around Button, his stride wasn't effortless and quick, but stilted and painful.

"He's barely putting weight on the front right paw," Lou observed aloud.

George leaned closer to the screen. "You're right. And look there, when he stops, he holds it off the ground completely."

"Should I call Noah?" Lou asked, feeling the urge to get up and go searching for the cat right away.

Sensing her urgency, Wesley said, "This was almost twenty-four hours ago. Hissie—er, Gullipurr could be anywhere in the county by now."

The man had a point. Lou raked her teeth over her lip as she thought about what their next steps might be. The surveillance video kept playing, and George bumped it back up to the faster speed.

Before Lou could come to any decision about what to do about Gullipurr, something on the video footage gained priority. Sneaking up to the florist was a group of… Lou squinted at the computer.

"Are those nuns?" George asked.

"Uh…" Lou wasn't sure what to say.

The people on the screen were dressed as nuns, all right. What wasn't clear was what they were doing in Brine at one o'clock in the morning.

A few seconds later, it became abundantly clear.

The three nuns used a rock from in front of the building to smash the window and break inside. A few minutes later, they raced out of the dark building, arms full of bouquets.

The three non-nuns staring at the computer screen fell silent as the video footage continued, now simply showing the broken window and empty parking lot.

"We've gotta get this to Easton," Lou whispered after a beat.

Wesley took over the mouse and clicked a few buttons. "Sure, I can send it to him."

George clicked her tongue, signaling that wouldn't work. "He and the other officers are a little more old-school," she said, standing. "They prefer if I put the files on a portable USB flash drive. I've got one in my car."

Returning Wesley's shocked look with a tilt of her eyebrows, George left to grab it.

The moment Lou was alone with Wesley, however, she snapped out of the trance they'd all been in since the confusing scene on the camera footage. A moment alone with Wesley was rare, and she needed to take advantage of it.

Turning to the young man, Lou said, "A cat? You have a cat, Wesley?" The words came out more biting and aggressive than she meant them to.

Wesley's head jerked back in surprise. "Uh, yeah?"

"George has spent months thinking you hate cats."

"Why would she think that?" A frown cut across Wesley's face.

Lou's cheeks heated. "Well, I mean… I guess I kind of gave her the idea back in February when you said you couldn't take Mr. Clawrcy."

Wesley's jaw clenched in frustration.

"Oh, don't give me that look. I thought you were going to tell her how you felt after we talked last. You're the one who refused to tell her the truth for months, and now it's too late because she's dating Austin." Lou swatted at his shoulder.

Offense furrowed his features at the motion.

But Lou was on a roll. "You know what? I think you're scared. I think you don't want to give her the chance to hurt you, so you waited around until someone else could swoop her up so you wouldn't have a choice. You lost her, but now you can blame it on Austin instead of your inaction."

"You really think I've lost her?" he whispered.

Lou softened her expression. "Look, I don't know. I

think she's convinced herself that Austin is who she needs to be with because she doesn't think you're interested. I would say that, regardless of what she does, you owe it to yourself to put the truth out there."

Wesley swallowed hard, but nodded. "I wasn't scared, by the way."

"What?"

His blue eyes met Lou's. "It wasn't that I was scared to tell her how I feel. I was going to … but then Figgy had a stroke in March, and we were in and out of the emergency room and the cardiologist a ton of times for the next few months. Between taking care of her, her medicine, her appointments, and keeping up with my work, I just didn't have the emotional energy."

Wesley's words were a punch to Lou's gut. She winced at yet another assumption gone wrong. *If only there was some catchy phrase to warn people against such things,* she thought to herself sarcastically.

"I'm… Gosh, I'm so incredibly sorry, Wesley. I feel like a jerk."

"Fig had just started doing better when I got the call from Austin to help with the thefts in the area. Then I saw George at the meeting and…" He shrugged.

"Wait." Lou inhaled. "Did you ask Austin to hire her and guarantee the two of you would have to work together?"

Wesley shook his head. "I promise, I didn't. That was all Austin. Though, I'm guessing that was before he became interested in dating her." At that statement, Wesley's features hardened.

"Sorry, again. But I don't think it's too late or anything.

The two of you should talk." She glanced at her phone. "In fact, I'm going to ask Noah to come pick me up so George can drive herself back. Okay?"

A bit of fear flashed behind Wesley's eyes at the prospect of putting himself out there. But along with the fear was determination. Lou placed a hand on his shoulder as she stood and called Noah, who was more than happy to come get her.

Lou was just walking outside to wait on Wesley's front porch when George scaled the front steps.

"I found it!" She brandished the small USB drive. "It was stuck between my seats. What's up?" George asked, eyes flicking from the house to Lou as if searching for answers.

"Noah's coming to pick me up."

"Is everything okay? Is it Marigold?" Worry gripped her questions.

"Everything's fine," Lou said quickly, not wanting to worry her friend. "But I think the two of you have some things to talk about."

George gripped the flash drive. With a hard swallow, she walked back inside Wesley's house.

CHAPTER 15

The next day was gorgeous, and Lou opted to run to work. She hadn't stopped thinking about poor Gullipurr and his limp. She hoped taking the long way around town would lead to a sighting.

Although she and Noah had driven around for an hour the night before, they'd seen neither fur nor whisker of the big cat.

Lou ran down as many side streets as she could. She zigzagged around Button, visiting all the places she'd seen him before, but finally had to call it quits. If she didn't turn toward the bookshop soon, she was going to be late opening.

Her day only went downhill from there. After roaming the shelves to make sure there wasn't another copy of *Gulliver's Travels* she'd missed, Lou studied each customer who entered, with the scrutiny and dedication she used to employ when editing a manuscript in her old New York City life. Again, the patrons noticed the behavior and often left without purchasing anything.

"You could always put a sign in the window that asks people to leave backpacks or large bags at the front of the shop," Cricket suggested.

"That feels like a big-city thing," Lou said. "If I did that in a small town like Button, I think I'd alienate my customers."

The older woman's eyes cut surreptitiously around the empty bookstore in a silent confirmation that the alienating-her-customers ship had already sailed. Even all her regulars hadn't shown up. And Lou had really been looking forward to catching up with George to see how her conversation with Wesley had gone.

But George didn't show. And with fewer and fewer customers, Lou took to spending her time posting a new blog entry about Gullipurr and his injuries, asking locals to contact her if they spotted him. After that, she cleaned the bookshop and took care of ordering for the following month.

The afternoon found her snuggled on the love seat with three of the foster cats, reading. Even though it was a Wednesday, usually a day she wouldn't dream of cutting short, she considered going home a couple of hours early.

Just as soon as the thought came to her, the front door opened. The bell ringing through the shop was the most lovely sound, and it caused her heart to flutter with excitement. She surged off the couch, only to freeze on the spot.

The customer who'd entered the shop was obviously a teenager. He was also a student at Silver Lake High School, based on the blue letterman jacket he wore. Her gaze narrowed on the backpack slung over one of his shoulders.

"Welcome in," Lou called in a strangled voice. "Uh, let me know if you need help finding anything."

The young man raised a hand in acknowledgment and then proceeded toward the new-release table. But he didn't seem to be looking at any of the books in front of him. His gaze flitted around the shop as he scowled at the genre signs Lou posted on the different aisles.

Lou's head felt light, possibly from standing up so quickly, or it could've been that her heart was beating dangerously fast. She would bet money that this kid had a special edition copy of *Gulliver's Travels* in that backpack. And now he was trying to figure out where to stash it.

Because of this assurance, Lou was unsurprised when the young man's attention locked on to the aisle sign for cookbooks, and he abandoned his poor act of browsing the new releases to walk toward it. It struck her as slightly odd since the last book had been found in the cookbook section, and they'd never repeated a hiding place before. Still, Lou followed, grabbing a stack of books to "shelve" so she could monitor him.

She peered around the corner, ducking back just as he nervously adjusted the strap of his backpack. Lou tensed. This was it. He was about to take a book out of that backpack and place it on the shelf. She was torn between letting him do it so she could check the note for the location and time of the next burglary or catching him in the act to confront him.

The fact that she was alone in the shop made the decision for her. She wasn't about to attempt the latter by herself. Whether the messengers were mere pawns or fully entrenched in the thievery, they had killed Heather, and Lou wasn't about to be next.

She slunk down the neighboring aisle, peering through openings in the bookshelf. But instead of taking anything out of his backpack, he slid a cookbook off the shelf and began paging through it. He self-consciously checked over his shoulder once more, but soon became enraptured by the recipes in the book. He stared at them as if he was trying to commit them to memory. Lou stayed close so she could see if he tried to take anything out of his bag, but he didn't. Instead, after flipping through a few more pages, he tucked the cookbook under one arm and headed for the checkout counter.

Lou scrambled back to the front of the store, smiling through her confusion as he handed over the book. It was titled *So You Think You're a Hopeless Cook?*

She must've spent too much time reading over the title because the kid shifted on his feet. "I ... uh ... There's this girl, and I"—he barked out a nervous laugh—"I wanted to cook her dinner."

Lou's heart softened. He was either the sweetest thing or a fantastic actor. But he hadn't left a book on the shelf, so it was plausible that his being a Silver Lake High School student was just a coincidence.

"Which dish are you thinking of making for her?" Lou asked, pivoting the book back toward him.

His eyes lit up, and he took the book back. He flipped through the pages for a moment before settling on a recipe and turning it so Lou could see. "I thought this one seemed romantic." He had the book open to a mushroom risotto recipe.

Lou wanted to wrap him up in a blanket and give him a mug of hot chocolate. He was precious.

"Oh, that's a great choice," she said.

Completely blowing any preconceived notions Lou had of the young man out of the water, he launched into a description of the girl he was hoping to impress. Genuine affection sparked in his eyes as he said, "She's nice to everyone, and I just want to do something nice for her, for a change. She's always thinking about other people."

Lou wanted to place her hand over her heart, but resisted the urge. "What made you come here instead of searching online or even going to Silver Lake Books?" Lou asked. "It's much closer to you, I'm guessing." She pointed to his letterman jacket.

He looked down at his outfit. "Oh, well, Tianna's a big reader, and she always says books are better than the internet, so I figured I'd start with one of these. Plus, I don't have a printer, so if I found a recipe on the internet, I'd have to keep pulling it up. I'm guessing I'm going to have to reread everything *a lot*," he admitted with a soft, awkward chuckle. "As for Silver Lake Books, they were closed. There was a note in the window about an emergency chamber of commerce meeting the owner needed to prepare for."

Surprise hit Lou like a slap to the face. She hadn't heard of there being another joint meeting. Was Silver Lake holding one of their own so soon? Pushing past her confusion, Lou scanned the book and placed it in a bag for the young man. As he paid, she studied him and realized it wasn't every day that she had a talkative high schooler at her disposal, especially not one who went to the very school she had so many questions about.

"How do you like Silver Lake High?" she asked, feigning as much indifference as she could muster.

He huffed out a laugh. "It's my senior year, so basically I'm Marshawn Lynch."

"Who?" Lou wrinkled her nose.

The boy looked at her blankly. "He used to play for the Seahawks. Famously said, 'I'm just here so I don't get fined.'" The kid studied her for any sign of recognition.

Lou's lips twisted in apology. "I'm not much of a sports follower."

He simply blinked as if he couldn't fathom such a concept.

But Lou still needed information about the school. "Can I ask about a few of your teachers?" Seeing that this was an exceptionally odd question to ask out of the blue, Lou added, "I'm considering donating some books to the high school, and I was wondering if I should talk to Mrs. Cowell, Miss Heller, or Miss Klegg about which books the school might need."

Fear flashed behind his eyes. "I wouldn't talk to Miss Heller if I were you. She's always mad." He glanced right, then left, before adding, "I kinda think it's because all she does is read poetry. That would make anyone cranky." He swallowed audibly. "Mrs. Cowell's nice, and she's, like, the boss of all the other English teachers. But Miss Klegg might take you up on some books about writing. Other than theater, her 'great love' is writing. She's always encouraging us to write our own novels or plays." He shrugged as if her enthusiasm hadn't rubbed off on him. "Actually, she might not be the best one to talk to right now because she's super busy putting on the final show of *As You Like It* this weekend. It's Shakespeare," he added, not knowing that was Lou's favorite of the bard's plays. "Tianna's not in this one, but she played a nun in *The Sound of Music* last year."

Lou felt like she'd swallowed a bug. Nun. Her thoughts returned to the nuns she'd seen on the surveillance footage of the florist break-in last night. Did that mean that Klegg was the person she was looking for, or did anyone who worked at the school have access to the theater costumes? Latching on to the only other thing she knew about the thieves—specifically the one who'd shot Heather—Lou decided to dig further.

"So, Miss Cowell's probably the one to talk to about the books, then. Gotcha. One more question. My, uh, friend was telling me about another teacher who works there. They're really tall. Do you know anyone who works there who's really tall?" Lou's heart ached as she thought, again, about Heather's death.

The kid scratched his cheek. "Our principal, Mr. Merton, isn't short but I wouldn't say he's tall either. Oh, our security officer is really tall. Although, I think some of his height has to do with the fact that he wears cowboy boots every day."

"Really?" Lou hadn't ever considered it, but she supposed the right boots would give a rather hefty boost to someone's height.

"Yeah, and he calls everyone 'partner.'" He grabbed his book. "Well, I've got to get going. Thanks."

Lou waved a goodbye to the kid. She chewed on her lip, considering the information she had gotten out of him about the teachers in question. If they could just find whoever had that bag with the pins on it, they might be able to get somewhere with this case. But that wasn't the only thing the kid had said that went through Lou's mind over the next few hours. He'd mentioned that Austin's store was closed for a chamber of commerce meeting. Odd. She hadn't heard anything about another meeting.

The rest of the day crawled by. Lou didn't have to worry about anyone trying to come in and plant the book because there weren't any customers. She closed the shop and took the cats upstairs to feed them, as she'd gotten into the habit of doing so she would know it wasn't them tripping the motion detector. Before she left, she cleaned their upstairs litter and replenished the water. While she worked, she felt her phone buzz with a notification that there was a movement in the bookshop, but with it going off throughout the day, she'd become all but numb to the alarms.

When she walked back downstairs, however, she realized that deciding not to check the camera might've been a mistake. There was something on the love seat in the center of the seating area that definitely hadn't been there when she'd gone upstairs.

It was roughly the size of a cat, but it wasn't one.

"Prudence?" Lou asked, her voice tight.

The terrifying doll didn't answer back—because, of course, she wouldn't. That would be incredibly concerning if she had. Concerning, like finding the doll inside the book-shop when she hadn't been there before.

Lou's body broke out in a cold sweat. She was just about to make a move—to run? She wasn't sure—when she heard a familiar chortle of laughter spill out from behind a book-shelf to her right.

Expression going flat, Lou turned toward the sound and crossed her arms. "Okaaay. You got me."

A cackling mass of dark waves and bronze skin rushed at Lou. Marigold wrapped her arms around Lou's stomach and hugged her tight. Grinning like a fool, Lou curled over the girl, wrapping her arms around her as well. She closed her eyes as she took in Marigold's summer scent. She smelled like blue skies, sunshine, and fresh air, which was especially potent after the softball practice she must've just come from, considering her outfit.

Noah stepped out from behind the same bookshelf Marigold had been hiding behind, answering the question of how she'd gotten inside the locked bookshop. His sheepish grin clarified that he'd been suckered into the prank rather than the mastermind behind it. The man really was wrapped around his daughter's finger, and Lou found it insanely attractive. She winked at him to show him there were no hard feelings. He lifted an arm and rested it against a bookshelf as his daughter continued to squeeze Lou within an inch of suffocation.

Marigold leaned back so she could beam up at Lou. "Was it a nice surprise?"

"You? Yes. Prudence? Less so." Lou gave the girl a showy cringe and shudder as she glanced at the doll.

"Dad thought you might need a little cheering up. He thought we could order pizza." Marigold chattered as if she hadn't been allowed to talk the entire day. A fact which Lou knew wasn't true, based on what her teacher had said during her spring parent-teacher conference.

"Oh, I'd love to join you." Lou shifted her gaze to Noah. "But I just found out there's another chamber of commerce meeting in Silver Lake this evening. I was thinking of stop-ping by to see what it's about." She wrapped an arm around Marigold's shoulders and jostled the girl. "As much as I'd rather eat pizza with you."

Marigold giggled, exaggerating the jostling by throwing her body from side to side, leaning her weight into Lou.

"Do you think they caught someone? Or learned infor-mation about the thefts?" Noah asked.

"Wesley or George would've told me if something that big had happened. I just want to go to the meeting to make sure it's nothing I need to know."

Noah took over holding up his still floppy daughter by hooking his arm around her back. "No problem. Did you run here this morning?" he asked.

"I did." Lou chewed on her lip. She hadn't considered that.

"Why don't you take my truck to Silver Lake?" He pulled out his keys and detached the fob for his truck. "Goldie and I can walk home, and that way, you don't have to worry about being late."

"Thank you." She leaned over to plant a kiss on his cheek. When she pulled back, she noticed Marigold leaning toward her, cheek tilted up, waiting for her own kiss. Lou let out a bright laugh. She placed her hands on either side of the girl's face and planted a loud raspberry of a kiss on her warm cheek.

Marigold giggled, squirming away. "We'll save you pizza, Lou."

Noah huffed out an affectionate chuckle before following the boisterous girl outside.

CHAPTER 16

Lou spent the next few minutes texting Willow and George to see if they'd heard anything about the impromptu meeting. Neither had.

Willow had a dressage show that weekend and really needed to spend the evening working with OC, so she declined. But George was interested. She said she'd meet Lou there since she was already in Brine. That piqued Lou's interest. Was George in Brine already because a certain blond private investigator lived there?

She'd waited all day for George to show up and give her an update about what had happened the night before, after she'd left Wesley's house. But George hadn't shown.

Suddenly, Lou wondered if her assurance that Wesley and George would fill her in if something big happened in the case wasn't presumptuous. Maybe something big had come up that had kept George in Brine all day, and neither she nor Wesley had thought to contact Lou.

She texted George directly, asking if anything had happened with the case that she should know about going into the meeting. But even though George had answered right away on the group thread, no answer came through to Lou's latter question.

So, it was either something George didn't want to text about, or she'd gotten busy.

Lou didn't have the time to wait, however, so she silenced her phone, locked up the bookstore, and headed out to Noah's truck. The drive to Silver Lake was quick, and she noted how the parking lot was packed, though not quite as much as the other night. Maybe this was simply a Silver Lake-only meeting. An odd wobble moved through Lou's gut, and she wondered what she might be about to walk into.

As it turned out, the answer to that was George. The young woman stood outside the large gymnasium, hiding behind the open double doors, and she stepped in front of Lou the moment she saw her. The one-woman barricade confused Lou for a moment, but then the din of chattering —and even some shouting—spilled out from the meeting and she froze.

"Why isn't Button here?" a woman's question cut through the rest, proving Brine had been invited along with Silver Lake.

Lou tucked herself behind the door, unable to see, but that didn't matter. She wanted to hear this. Convinced that Lou wasn't about to barge inside, George leaned into the wall next to her to listen as well.

"Okay," Austin's voice rose above the crowd. "We'd love to answer your questions, but in order to do that, we can't have people yelling and holding side conversations. Please let us explain. You'll see that Ian is setting up a microphone over to the right. If you still have questions when we're done, you're free to form a line behind that, and we'll get to as many as we can."

Lou released the air in her lungs. Austin's calm, competent demeanor even made her feel better … for a moment.

"Much better," Austin said once the crowd quieted. "First of all, we didn't invite the Button chamber members this time, at the request of Jessica Stoneking. I'll let her come up and explain her concerns herself."

There was a brief pause as Jessica took Austin's place.

"Hi, everyone. I'm Jessica. I own the Silver Ridge Bar and Grill, and I hoped we could have a meeting to discuss the Button problem."

At that, Lou's forehead creased. Her gaze swept to George, who was mouthing, "Problem?" while making a similarly confused face.

"For those of you who haven't heard yet, Louisa Henry, the owner of the Button bookstore, has been hiding the fact that the thieves have been using her shop to communicate for weeks."

Gasps rang out from the group.

Jessica pushed on. "They've been leaving the location and time of each theft right under her nose about a day before the break-ins happen, and she's kept it from us."

Lou's brain swam with the cacophony of noise that followed. She wasn't overly surprised the information had gotten out. It wasn't as if she was hiding it, and her regulars—as much as she loved them—were each terrible gossips. What surprised her was that anyone would hear that and jump to the conclusion that she was helping the thieves.

Once Jessica got the chamber members calm enough to proceed, one voice sounded above the rest.

"That's unfair. She told the police. She's been handing over anything she finds."

Wesley.

"The police?" Jessica asked, the sneer that must've been on her face clear in her tone. "You mean the man she lives next to and is close friends with?"

Wesley scoffed. "Like that matters. But even if it did, Detective West has been working with the Brine and Silver Lake Police Departments as well. No one is hiding anything."

"Then why haven't we heard about this? Why didn't she tell us during the last meeting?" Jessica asked. Lou could picture the woman putting a hand on her hip.

"Because she didn't even realize what was happening until after we last met," Wesley said, his voice adopting a clipped quality.

Gratitude swelled in Lou. Laid-back, unflappable Wesley was fiercely defending her. Based on the way George's hand moved to her chest, as if attempting to still her heart, Lou wasn't the only one affected by the display of loyalty.

"Does anyone else find it suspicious that they're using her bookstore to communicate?" a man called out, receiving a chorus of agreement.

"Why wouldn't they just text one another?" another person asked.

Lou could hear Wesley's sigh of exasperation all the way out in the hallway.

"It has to be linked to her," a woman shouted. "I heard

she's from New York City. Do we even know why she moved here?"

"Because her husband died suddenly and tragically, and she wanted to be close to her best friend." Wesley's terse voice rose above the rest.

The crowd went momentarily silent.

"Did she kill her husband?" someone asked.

Shock swept through the room in whispers and exclamations.

"Are you going to do anything about this?" Wesley asked, presumably to Austin, because, a moment later, he started speaking again.

"Okay, let's settle down."

But Lou had heard enough. She turned and walked out to the parking lot.

George jogged behind her. "Lou, I'm… That was awful. I don't blame you for leaving."

"I'm not upset," she said, turning to face her friend so she could see the truth behind her statement. "They're scared and don't have another explanation for what's happening, so they're latching on to the first thing that makes even the slightest bit of sense. I'm okay with being their scapegoat for now." She exhaled a breathy laugh. "I don't particularly want to stay and listen, but I don't really care what a bunch of strangers think."

George puffed out her cheeks.

A vibration began in Lou's purse as her phone rang. She scowled at the unknown number, and was about to send the call to voicemail—it was likely just a telemarketer—but something stopped her. She answered.

"Hello, is this Lou?" an old man's voice wobbled through the phone.

"It is. May I ask who's calling?"

He let out a breath of relief. "Oh, good. This is Pete Inslee. I follow your *Gullipurr's Travels* blog and I saw your latest post about the poor guy possibly being hurt. You said to call the number you included if we saw him, so hopefully you can get him some help." Pete coughed. "I wanted to let you know that I just saw him."

Any negative emotions lingering from what she'd overheard at the chamber of commerce meeting flitted away, replaced by hope.

"Oh, Pete. That's wonderful news."

George arranged her expression into a question.

"Where did you see Gullipurr?" Lou asked, hoping that would fill George in on the topic of the call.

"He just cut through my backyard. I live in Brine, on Relish Road."

A laugh almost sputtered out of Lou at the serious way Pete said the silly name of his road, but Lou knew Button had little room to criticize. At least their street names were cute, not named after pickles. Pete's information was more important than anything, so she held it together.

The man cleared his throat. "He was still limping, like you said in your post. I hope you can help him."

"I'll do my best. Thank you so much, Pete."

They hung up, and Lou turned toward George. "Someone just spotted Gullipurr in Brine," she explained. "I'm going to try to catch him and bring him to Noah. Want to come?"

"I can't. I actually came here to see someone." George

looked over her shoulder as Wesley stormed out of the building.

"Wesley?" Lou whispered.

But George shook her head just as Wesley caught sight of them, and his brows drew together in concern. He jogged in their direction.

"No, I was actually here for—" George didn't finish that statement, because Austin came rushing after Wesley. "Austin," she breathed out his name.

Lou's lips parted in understanding.

"Wesley, wait," Austin called. "I'm sorry about that. I—" It was at that moment that Austin clocked Lou's presence. His cheeks flushed red. "Lou, y-you weren't in there, were you?"

Wesley turned to George and Lou, eyes wide, as if he hadn't thought of that possibility.

"You mean, did I hear everyone talking about how I probably killed my husband and must be behind this whole thing since the thieves are using my bookstore as some sort of messaging station? Definitely not," Lou deadpanned.

George cut a quick glance at Wesley, who looked down at his shoes.

"I'm so sorry. I'm trying to get it under control." Austin placed a hand on George's arm, cradling her elbow.

The touch was intimate in a way Lou hadn't expected. And she wasn't the only one who seemed to think that. Wesley's gaze lifted from the ground, stuck on the point of contact between George and Austin. His hand twitched at his side, and Lou could've sworn the movement mirrored that of Darcy in the famous hand-flex scene from the *Pride and Prejudice* movie.

"You don't mind waiting, do you?" Austin asked George. "I know we had plans, but I think this will take just a little longer. I didn't expect that it would get this out of control."

"I can wait," George said

Nodding, Austin finally let his hand fall away from her arm. "I'm really sorry, Lou. I'm going to fix this." With that, he jogged back inside.

And then Lou was left with two people who didn't seem to want to meet each other's eyes, and definitely weren't saying anything.

"Well, I'm going to try to find Gullipurr," she announced, breaking the awkward silence. But she couldn't look away from the devastation on Wesley's features. "Wesley, why don't you join me?"

He lifted his eyebrows along with his gaze. "Really?"

"Who couldn't use a private investigator when tracking down a slippery, injured feline?" Lou elbowed him.

That elicited a slight lift of one corner of his mouth. "Okay."

Lou turned toward George. "See you tomorrow?" she asked, but there was a force behind her words that she hoped would convey that she wanted to talk to her about all of this, to get the scoop on what was going on.

"Yeah. See ya tomorrow," George croaked out, barely lifting her eyes.

When Wesley suggested he drive, Lou declined. There was already a cat crate in the back of Noah's truck—that was the reason she gave him. But the real reason she declined? Wesley's lowered Honda Civic looked like it went one speed, and one speed only: screaming fast.

They climbed inside the truck's cab and Lou entered the destination into her phone. "This is also perfect because the guy who called was from Brine, so you can help me since you know the town so well."

Wesley blinked at her. "Wait. The cat thing is real? I thought you just made that up to save me back there."

"Of course the cat is real." Lou backed out of the parking spot and started toward Brine. "And in the time it takes us to get to Brine, I need to hear about what happened between you and George."

CHAPTER 17

esley blew out a long breath—so long, in fact, that Lou glanced over in disbelief at one point, surprised by his lung capacity.

"So? Did you tell her how you felt, last night?" Lou asked when he didn't start talking.

She did her best to keep her eyes on the road, but she stole a few looks his way in the seconds that followed.

"I did," he said, finally.

"You did?"

"Yeah." Wesley sank farther into the passenger seat. "I told her about how I haven't been able to stop thinking about her, about how I'm not interested in anyone else because they don't challenge me like she does, and I told her I wanted to try giving us a second chance. I even promised that if she went on another date with me, I would definitely make it to the end. Well, at least through the entrées."

Lou scowled over at him.

He put his hands up in defense. "It was a joke. She knew it was a joke. She laughed."

None of that made sense. If Wesley had bared his soul to George, why was she making plans with Austin?

Lou continued to dig. "But then … what? What did she say after that?"

"She said that she appreciated me telling her and asked if she could have some time to think about it." He lifted his hands but let them drop into his lap.

"That's it?"

"Yup."

"And today, she's obviously going out with Austin," Lou said, more to herself than to Wesley, but he answered anyway.

Well, he didn't verbally answer. What he did was mime a knife plunging into his heart.

Lou grimaced.

He must have noticed her expression because he said, "No, it's okay. She's not obligated to return my feelings. She was already committed to Austin, and I missed my chance. Heck, maybe even before Austin, it still might have been a no." He swallowed, as if the idea was hard to admit. "But you were right, Lou. I do feel better having told her the truth. Keeping that inside was too much. Don't get me wrong; at first it was fun. Riling her and wondering if she liked it as much as I did—that was exhilarating. But once I'd admitted to myself how I actually felt about George, the wondering if she could ever love me back started to become a little unhealthy." He snorted out a humorless laugh. "Last month, I took the unhealthiness to a new level and watched a bunch of romance movies as some sort of outlet for my feelings. I think I watched that Keira Knightly version of *Pride and Prejudice* half a dozen times."

Lungs jolting, Lou said, "I thought I recognized that hand flex back there!"

"Yeah, I got really good at it after my third or fourth time through," he admitted sheepishly.

"Wesley, watching *Pride and Prejudice* isn't unhealthy. It's one of the most beautiful, enduring love stories in the world. It's a masterpiece—both versions," she added. When he shot her a confused look, she added, "There are some people who are die-hard fans of the Keira Knightly version, and others who prefer the Colin Firth miniseries. And then there are those of us who are happy to watch either, or to reread the book. Either way, people use movies like that to experience emotions, and that's a good thing to be die hard about."

Wesley looked wistful for a moment, and Lou thought she'd really gotten through to him about leaning into his emotions when he said, *"Die Hard*, now that's a fantastic movie."

Rolling her eyes, Lou let out a groan.

Mistaking her groan as a reaction to his circumstance, Wesley said, "It's okay, Lou. Maybe I'm not meant to find my Lizzy. Maybe I'm just the 'excellent boiled potatoes' guy." He used a haughty British accent as he repeated the iconic line.

Lou burst into laughter at that. "You're not Mr. Collins, Wesley, but you are right about one thing. George has to decide now. That's a very mature way to see it. You've done your part, and I'm proud of you."

At that point, the streets began to have increasingly pickle-themed names, and Lou kept her eyes peeled for the house Pete had described. Wesley told her where to park, and they went out to search on foot. Lou grabbed the spare cat crate Noah kept in the back of his truck, just in case.

Peter, as it turned out, lived in a house between Relish Road and Bread and Butter Lane, a fact that made Lou wheeze with laughter until Wesley pointed to the Brine pickle factory across the street and said he'd often seen groups of stray cats hanging out by the dumpsters in the back. She remembered why they were here—to help Gullipurr—and grew serious once more.

They crossed Relish Road, and Wesley led Lou around to the back of the pickle factory. The factory was closed for the day, so they didn't have to worry about running into any workers, wondering what the two were doing lurking around. But that was where their good luck ended.

Gullipurr wasn't there.

They were about to go over to Pete's, to knock on his door and ask him to describe what direction Gullipurr had gone, when something in one of the factory's many dumpsters caught Lou's eye. About twenty gorgeous flower bouquets had been tossed on the top of the other garbage. Well, they used to be gorgeous. Now their petals were bent, their stems broken, and everything was browning as they lay among the trash after a hot day or two in the sun.

Lou's gaze narrowed, and her eyes flashed to Wesley, who'd walked over to her side to see what had caught her attention. "What do you want to bet that these are the same ones we saw the thieves stealing from the Brine florist the other night?"

"Well, maybe they realized reselling fresh flowers isn't the easiest thing to do," Wesley suggested.

But Lou set down the cat crate she was holding so she could use one of the bouquets to push another out of the way. "Look." She pointed to the bottom of the dumpster, where one of the expensive cashmere sweaters from Heather's clothing boutique was sadly now covered in dumpster grime. "That's what they stole from Heather's place the night they shot her."

"So, they're not trying to resell what they steal? Any of it?" Wesley scratched his temple. "Then why do any of it? Why risk it? This isn't a light misdemeanor anymore. They murdered a woman."

Lou shook her head, but something one person called out at the chamber of commerce meeting stuck in her mind. "Me," she whispered.

"Don't listen to them," Wesley scoffed. "They're just searching for someone to blame."

She'd told George the same thing. But that comment had struck a chord inside her mind, one she couldn't help but hear ringing louder as this new piece of evidence strengthened the possibility. It didn't hurt that Silas had already mentioned it days earlier.

"Think about it," she told Wesley. "I was the first business hit. They're using my shop as a headquarters, in a sense. Anywhere in Silver Lake would make much more sense for that since it's equidistant to Button and Brine. They're stealing things—*things,* not money. And then tossing the things away because they don't need the money. That's not what it's about. It's about me. It's about making everyone doubt me." Her voice drifted quieter as her words rang truer, the sensation of rightness moving from her brain to her heart.

"But, why?"

"I don't know, but Easton's gotta see this. The Brine police have to know what's happening too." She pulled out her phone and was about to call Easton when an orange blur ran across the back lot—limped was more like it. He was nowhere near as fast as he'd been before his injury. "Gullipurr!"

The cat stopped in its tracks, making eye contact with Lou.

"Does he know his name?" Wesley whispered the question.

"It kinda seems like he does." She stretched her hand forward, making kissing sounds and *pspspsps* sounds, and every other sound that had ever gotten a cat to pay her any attention.

Gullipurr crouched lower. Lou halted any forward movement.

"Wesley, move around behind him," she instructed through a measured whisper, returning to where she'd set down the cat crate.

As Wesley followed her instructions, Lou opened the crate. She wished she'd thought of bringing a can of wet food or something enticing for the guy, but she supposed the warm blanket at the bottom of the crate was going to have to be enough of an incentive. Gullipurr's eyes were enormous as he crouched low, glancing behind him at Wesley and then back at Lou.

Even in the crouch position, his right paw trembled, and he shifted its position. He was definitely in pain. That fact became even clearer as Wesley approached from behind Gullipurr, and instead of running, the cat simply flattened himself to the ground more.

Wesley's fingers clasped around the scruff of the cat's neck at the same moment that Lou moved forward with the crate. Gullipurr must've known he needed help because the cat surged forward out of Wesley's grip, right into the crate. Wesley shut the door behind him.

"Okay," he said, expelling a puff of air. "What do we do now?"

Lou made sure the door was secured before picking up the crate. "We take him to Noah and figure out what's wrong with his leg." She glanced sidelong at the young man, sure he'd rather be doing something else with his Wednesday night. "Or I can take him. You don't need to come with if you have other things to do."

"The woman I'm crazy about is out with another man tonight. I'm definitely coming along. If I don't have this, I'll just end up watching Elizabeth and Darcy fall in love again," he mumbled.

"Right. Let's get this guy back to Button, then. We can call Easton on the way."

NOAH AND MARIGOLD met Lou and Wesley at the veterinary clinic, bringing with them the promised leftover pizza, to Wesley's delight. Noah took Gullipurr to the back, leaving Wesley and Marigold in the waiting room.

Marigold, who'd never formally met Wesley, was immediately entranced by him. Lou didn't blame the girl. Wesley asked her questions about her life and appeared genuinely interested in the answers. He also started a game where he spun her around the room, one that began a mere half hour after they'd met one another and resurfaced every few minutes. Marigold needed time to regain her equilibrium in between.

While Wesley entertained Marigold, Lou slipped into the back to help Noah with Gullipurr. She acted as his technical assistant as he examined the cat after giving him a dose of pain medication to make him more amenable to being poked and prodded. But they quickly found the issue.

"It looks like he had a few cuts that got infected." Noah pushed back Gullipurr's fur so Lou could see a grouping of nasty gashes along the right paw, moving up to his armpit. "This one here has turned into an abscess." Noah indicated the wound closest to the cat's body. "It was likely the hardest for him to clean because of its position."

"We can help him, though, right?" Lou asked.

"Absolutely. Medication and rest will see him as good as new." Noah patted the cat's head.

Gullipurr was either really feeling the drugs, or understood they were there to help, because he blinked sleepily, much more relaxed than he had been earlier.

Lou helped Noah clean out the wounds and administer the medication before they bandaged him up and set him up in the back to rest while he healed.

That taken care of, Lou and Noah rejoined Wesley and Marigold, who were in the middle of a rollicking game of I-spy in the waiting room, which included running up and touching everything before being allowed to guess it. Noah beamed, watching how good Wesley was with the girl, but Lou's heart hurt at the reminder that Gullipurr wasn't the only one left wounded after today. George had made her decision. Lou hoped Wesley's emotional wounds would be as easy to heal.

CHAPTER 18

The next day, Lou waited impatiently for George to show up at the bookstore. She did her opening chores with the cats, made small talk with her other regulars, and navigated the busier than usual traffic that morning, all while keeping a keen eye on the front door.

The other regulars filtered out over the course of the morning, and Lou was just about to send George a text when she ambled into the bookstore. She collapsed onto the floor in a tired heap, cats immediately surrounding her.

Lou tried to wait, but she couldn't hold in the question. "How was your date with Austin last night?" She kept her voice down since there were a handful of customers in the shop at the moment.

George didn't answer at first, instead focusing on giving each of the shop cats a thorough hello, complete with chin scratches and top-of-the-head kisses. Finally, she shot Lou a smirk. "Louisa Henry, are you prying?"

"Me?" Lou placed a hand on her collarbone. "Never." She couldn't help the laugh that burst out of her after the lie.

"It wasn't a date," George said flatly. "I wanted to tell him, in person, that I can't see him anymore."

"Because?" Lou asked.

George glanced up at Lou in exasperation. "I'm pretty sure you know why, Miss 'I think the two of you need to talk.'"

Lou held back a smile. "Yes, but I'd really like to hear it from you."

"Fine. I don't want to date Austin anymore because Wesley told me he has feelings for me. He has for a while, just as long as I've had them for him. Which is good because my quashing wasn't exactly going great."

Lou eyed her, pausing to greet a customer who entered and to answer a question for yet another. Once that was taken care of, Lou turned back to George. "And you're no longer convinced he'll be bad for you? Because you were pretty adamant before that he wasn't what you wanted."

"I only said that because I thought he didn't want me," George scoffed. "It was a defense mechanism to protect my heart when I thought he didn't share my feelings."

"Okay." Lou accepted the answer. "One more question."

George flicked both brows up, waiting.

"Why doesn't Wesley know any of this?"

A blush overtook George's face. "Because I wanted to talk to Austin first. To break things off with him before admitting anything to Wesley. Because I know the moment I do, I'm going to want to kiss him again, and I don't want to string along Austin. He's a nice guy."

"Admirable." Lou grabbed a stack of books to reshelve. "But you know this isn't olden times. It's not like you've been promised to Austin or anything, nor are the two of you in a committed, long-term relationship. You went on one date."

"Yes, I know that. And if I knew it was going to be this difficult to talk to him about it, I wouldn't have made this stipulation up in my mind." George sighed.

"You mean, you haven't broken it off with Austin yet?" Lou stopped mid-movement, a book hanging precariously off the shelf.

"Well, it was kind of hard to when he was stuck in that meeting for two hours. By the time everyone left, he looked exhausted and asked if we could switch our date to tonight. He wanted to go to dinner, but I told him I'd meet him at Silver Lake Books at closing time. I want to tell him right away, so I don't string him along anymore."

Lou tapped the spine of the book, settling it in its rightful spot in between the others. "Going to another bookstore. I see how it is," she joked.

"His doesn't have cats, which is the biggest drawback for me. You know that." George gazed fondly at the feline fosters surrounding her.

A customer sidled up to the counter. "I'm sorry. Were the two of you just talking about Silver Lake Books?"

Lou's attention snapped up, not having noticed the woman's closeness. She nodded warily.

"That's who told us to come here," she said. "The owner all but shooed us out of his own store. Had to close for a few hours for some reason." She frowned, as if she was just now wondering what that reason might be. "Anyway, when a few people complained, he said that Whiskers and Words in Button was a great place to find everything we needed."

Lou and George exchanged a knowing glance.

"Austin's a very nice guy," George said wholeheartedly.

The woman agreed and left to peruse the shelves with the rest of the crowd.

Shoulders slumping forward, Lou sighed. "What do you want to bet that Austin didn't actually need to close? He just felt bad that I overheard that meeting yesterday and he sent a bunch of business my way."

George got to her feet, only to sink into one of the chairs around the front table. "Yep. Sounds like something he'd do."

Lou studied her. "Are you having second thoughts about breaking up with the guy?"

"No," George said, resolutely. "He's wonderful. And he'll be amazing for someone else. But it's not fair to him for me to continue in a relationship when I have such strong feelings for Wesley."

"Who's also wonderful, by the way." Lou nudged George with her elbow, eliciting a smile.

"He is," she agreed. "Did he tell you about Fig's stroke?" Her eyes welled up like she might cry. When Lou nodded, George added, "That's why he wasn't around the past few months. I thought he was avoiding me." She snorted. "That'll teach me to make everything all about myself."

Lou exhaled. "The longer I live, the more I learn I'm rarely the reason for other people's behavior. We're so important to ourselves that sometimes it's hard not to make it all about us."

George grinned. "Well, I'd better get going. I've got a few appointments today before I go talk to Austin." She sent Lou a wave over her shoulder and slipped out the front door, holding it open for another large group of shoppers.

The crowds lasted right until closing time. Before she locked the front door, Lou took one last happy turn about the bookshop to reassemble a few things and straighten books customers had left askew. She hadn't realized how much she'd missed having a full bookshop until today.

Any feelings of happiness leached out of her the moment she spotted a copy of *Gulliver's Travels* sitting on the historical fiction bookshelf at just about eye level.

It had been so crowded that she hadn't been able to follow everyone around—nor had she wanted to, honestly. Not constantly looking at her customers as threats had been so nice for a change. But it seemed she'd paid the price. Her fingers shook with barely restrained frustration as she reached for the copy.

A piece of paper stuck out from the middle like a bookmark.

Lou pulled it out, eyes poring over the text.

He angled his
body toward her. She
was lavender and
lollipops—flowery and
sweet. And she loved
him. He just wished
he loved her back.
The old him might've
wanted someone nice,
but his tastes had
changed. He needed
anger, spice, and
danger. If he was
going to commit to
one woman, it was
going to be out of
fear.

Wrinkling her nose at both the concept and the prose, Lou rushed over to her checkout counter to grab a pen. She circled the lower letters and rewrote them below.

He angled his
body toward her. She
was lavender and
lollipops-flowery and
sweet. And she loved
him. He just wished
he loved her back.
The old him might've
wanted someone nice,
but his tastes had
changed. He needed
anger, spice, and
danger. If he was
going to commit to
one woman, it was
going to be out of
fear.

games and gifts

Games and gifts. That was it. No time included on this one.

She called Easton.

"Another one?" he guessed, in lieu of a greeting.

"Yep. It says Games and Gifts. I'm thinking it's Smartie's in Silver Lake."

Smartie's Games and Gifts was a great store that carried puzzles, science kits, and other educational items, perfect for kids.

She swallowed. "There's no time on this one. They're getting even more cryptic."

Easton sighed. "I'll be there in a few."

They hung up and Lou texted Noah, explaining that she was going to be at the shop a little longer before heading home. Knowing he'd wonder why, she sent a follow-up text.

Found another book.

I'll come to you. Be there soon.

Just knowing he was going to be there made her feel better. He and Easton arrived moments apart, and Lou was just about to lock the front door when she caught sight of Willow walking her way down the street. She held the door open for her too.

"Hey," Willow said. "I was just going to see if you wanted to grab some ice cream together before we go home." Her gaze snagged on Easton and Noah already inside the bookshop. "Buuut, it seems as if we've got more important things to discuss." She scooted through the open door.

Lou closed it behind her. "I found another book. The code mentions a place in Silver Lake, but no time is listed."

"You didn't see who might've left it?" Easton asked.

Her head hung as she shook it. "I was swamped today."

"We can watch through the security footage tonight." Noah placed a hand over hers.

She smiled gratefully. "I know this is going to sound paranoid, but…" She hated what she was about to say, but she needed to voice her fear to someone other than Wesley. "At the risk of making this about me, this really seems personal, like it's directed at me."

No one said anything, but from the pain in her friends' eyes as they watched her, they couldn't disagree.

"They're using my shop. The locals are asking questions." Lou rubbed her hands over her face. "I'm wondering if I shouldn't close for a few days to see if it stops them."

She expected Easton to argue with her, to tell her she was overreacting. Instead, he said, "I think that might be for the best, honestly. If you can swing it."

"I was planning on closing for a few hours on Saturday to go watch Willow and OC at their show, anyway. What's a whole day, plus Friday?" she asked rhetorically, knowing very well that they were her biggest money-making days. She mustered a small smile in order to seem more convincing.

Noah hugged her to him. "We'll figure this out."

She turned her attention to Easton. "Find anything on those three teachers we sent you?"

"Nope. We questioned each one, but they all said they've never stepped foot inside your bookstore, nor did they admit to having any connection to any of the thefts," he said. "One of them is obviously lying, but I can't exactly look into them more than that without a warrant, and one of them was particularly scary, so I know she'd fight us if we didn't have the proper documentation." Easton shook himself in a shiver.

Lou chuckled. "Ah, that must've been Miss Heller. She teaches creative writing, and according to a student I met, she's cranky as all get-out." Her eyes widened as she thought about the young man from the other day. He'd known so much about the teachers, so much more than Easton had been able to find out by asking them directly. "What if we go to the source?" she suggested. "If we can at least figure out which one has that tote bag. If we can link the bag with her and show a judge the video footage. That might be enough to get her to talk, right?"

Easton blew out his cheeks. "I mean, sure. But what do you mean, go to the source?"

"Yeah, we can't exactly waltz into a high school uninvited," Willow pointed out. She would know, having been a high school teacher up until last year.

Lou snapped her fingers. "No, but we could go to the play they're putting on this Saturday evening." She hadn't been able to help herself. She'd looked it up after the young man had left her shop the other day. It was her favorite Shakespeare play, after all. There had still been plenty of tickets available.

She held each one of her friends' gazes for a moment before they all agreed. And even though the thought of being connected to the thefts and being forced to close because of it made a terrible feeling sink into the pit of her stomach, having a plan in place gave her a sliver of hope.

CHAPTER 19

That sense of hope slipped right through Lou's fingers the next morning when she heard the news that the candy shop in Button had been robbed the night before.

"But the code said gifts and games," Lou argued with Cricket, the unfortunate messenger of the news.

Even though Whiskers and Words was closed for the day, Lou had run into one of her regulars on the street after grabbing a coffee. There was a small crowd gathered around the candy shop across the street as people whispered about the broken window and what the thieves had made away with.

"They've tricked you before," Cricket said with a jerk of her shoulders. "Who's to say that wasn't just some way to mess with you again?"

At that news, Lou crossed the street to her bookshop, needing some place safe to deal with the news, to process the feelings that she'd let everyone down, yet again. She busied herself with feeding the cats and making sure they had clean water and tidy litter boxes, of course. But she also found herself wandering through the shop, running her fingers over the books, missing being there, especially on a Friday.

She lingered less on Saturday morning, mostly because she had a horse show to get to, and Willow's dressage test was fairly early.

Before she left, however, Lou walked through the romance section of the shop, a blank spot on the shelf catching her eye. She slotted her finger into the place where the thin horror book had been placed without her knowledge.

Rushing over to her checkout counter, Lou pulled the book from the drawer she'd stuffed it in when George had brought it to her attention last week.

Was it possible that the paragraphs she'd been reading in the notes tucked inside copies of *Gulliver's Travels* had come from this book? Was that why they were eerily familiar?

It was in book form, but if it had been printed on demand by the author through one of the smaller self-publishing companies, it might not show up on the plagiarism sites she was using.

Flipping through it in search of the different paragraphs, however, proved almost too much for Lou. Before opening it, she had fleetingly wondered if she'd been too harsh on the book. Her memory might've blown the violence and gore out of proportion, as memories tended to do. But as she read snippets from the pages, scanning for anything similar to the typewritten messages with the embedded codes, she realized she'd been right to be horrified. It was incredibly, gratuitously violent, especially toward the women characters. She pushed through, however, trying to find the exact text from the papers she'd found.

She looked as long as she could, until she felt a little nauseated, right up to the minute she needed to leave for Willow's horse show. Lou tucked the book into her purse and headed home to pick up Noah and Marigold.

Their arrival at the local barn where the event was taking place was a whirlwind of locating Willow's truck and trailer, fussing over how wonderful OC looked with his mane and tail braided, and wishing Willow luck on her test.

After that, they wandered over to the stands, selecting seats that would give them a perfect view of Willow and OC. They had to wait for a few other competitors to go first, and while Marigold was absolutely entranced by the horses, Noah must've gotten bored because he started looking around.

"What's this?" he asked, a shadow moving over his face as he slipped the terrifying book out of Lou's bag.

Lou snorted in surprise. "Oh, that." She kept the cover angled away from Marigold, not wanting to traumatize the poor girl. "George found that on my romance shelf a week or so back. Apparently, the other bookstores in the area have them, too, but the author, at least, asked them to carry his book. With me, he just slipped it onto a shelf, and not even the right one."

Shooting a worried glance at the terrifying cover, Noah asked, "And you're reading it?" His question was tentative.

"Definitely not," she blurted. A laugh shivered out of her. "Well, not on purpose. I got a wild idea today that the excerpts from the coded messages in the Gulliver books might've come from this one. You know, yet another book slipped onto my shelves without my permission or knowledge." She snorted. "Each time I read one of them, there's something so familiar about them, like I've read the lines before. And the author of this book definitely doesn't seem to like or understand women, which fits with the few type-written paragraphs I've read. I thought they might be from here, and that's why I recognized them."

"Are they?" Noah asked, taking it from her and thumbing through the typewritten papers she was using as a collective bookmark.

"Not that I can find," Lou admitted.

"What's that?" Marigold asked, finally tearing her focus from the competition at the sight of the one thing that could get her to look away from horses: a book.

Lou snatched it away from Noah and clutched it to her chest. "Uh, something you definitely don't want to read. It's very scary."

Marigold's nose wrinkled, and she leaned away as if the book might snap out and bite her. "Like Prudence scary? Or real scary?" she asked, showing how much she was enjoying the creepy doll her grandmother had given her and the silly games they were playing with her.

Slipping it back into her purse, Lou said, "Real scary." She widened her eyes, and Marigold nodded somberly.

George arrived with Wesley in tow a few moments later. Lou kept her grin contained as much as she could. Seeing the two of them together felt like a long time coming. Lou realized it was probably how people had felt about her and Noah when they'd finally opened up about their relation-ship. Marigold greeted Wesley like a celebrity, practically jumping on him as she begged him to start up a new game of I-spy with her, but Easton came over to join them, a signal that Willow's test was up next, so they all quieted down.

While many other members of the audience displayed nervous energy, fidgeting before their competitor came into the ring, Willow's guests were calm. They knew the tireless hours of practice she and OC had put in to get to this point. Also, Willow only did these shows for fun, to give her something to train for. It didn't matter to her if they placed or not.

Unsurprisingly, she and OC nailed each one of the difficult moves, making the same test they'd seen other horse and rider combinations struggle through look easy. Lou took videos throughout the morning to send to her nieces, especially of the part where Willow and OC placed first.

After the award ceremony, they met Willow and OC at her trailer, pulling her into tight hugs and planting kisses of congratulations on OC's velvety nose.

Willow practically glowed as she removed the saddle and bridle from OC, placing them in the trailer. She slid Marigold onto his back while she finished brushing him off. That was where Cassidy found them a short while later, when she came to pick up Marigold. They slid the girl off the horse's back and handed over her schoolbag, since she'd be staying with Cass the whole weekend.

A conspiratorial look passed between Lou, Noah, and Marigold. Prudence was tucked inside the backpack and would find her way into one of Cassidy's closets before the weekend was over.

"Okay, now that Marigold's gone, do you want to tell us

more about this plan of yours, Lou?" George asked, referring to the somewhat cryptic text Lou had sent her on Thursday evening, inviting her to the play.

"Sure. Our high school visit will be twofold," she explained. "The first aim is to find evidence of the tote bag with all the pins on it that I saw the woman carrying that day she came into my shop. There are three teachers and three couples, so we should split up when we get there. I say we look in their classrooms first."

Lou remembered when Ben had been a professor. His office had been separate from the classrooms he taught in, mostly because other professors also utilized the space. But at the elementary, middle, and high school levels, teachers usually had a designated classroom that doubled as their office space, just as Willow had back when she'd taught horticulture at Button High.

"And what if the classrooms are locked?" Easton narrowed his eyes, obviously still not sold on the idea.

"Then we move on to the second aim," Lou said. "The students and families know a lot about these teachers. Most of the audience will probably be made up of that population. If we can, chat with people sitting nearby about your assigned teacher. Where does she spend her free time? Maybe even ask about the bag. Has anyone heard of costumes going missing? Stuff like that. It can't hurt."

The group nodded along. Easton looked reluctant but glad to hear that they would not be breaking any laws.

"Which teacher should we take?" George asked.

"Why don't you and Wesley take Miss Heller?"

"The grumpy one who only reads poetry?" George

scoffed, remembering what Lou had told her about the woman.

"She likely won't be there tonight. Neither will Mrs. Cowell." Lou turned her attention to Willow and Easton. "You two will take her. She's the head of the English department. Noah and I will take the hardest one since this is my idea."

Noah put a hand on her lower back in support.

"The drama teacher is going to be surrounded tonight, and her classroom will likely be crowded with students before the play." Easton said what everyone was thinking.

"Exactly." Lou winced. "Anyone want to switch?"

They all laughed. Then they made plans to meet at the high school an hour before the play was set to begin since Lou had already purchased their tickets online.

Willow checked her watch. "Good, that gives me time to get this guy home and shower." She tugged at her fitted dressage outfit. "I'm sweating like crazy." She peeled out of the jacket, leaving her in a white sleeveless button-up.

"We'll see you there. We're off to redo our first date," Wesley said with a smirk as he looked at George, who pressed her lips together to hide a smile.

"Hopefully we'll actually make it longer than five minutes this time," George said.

Lou had no doubt they would.

She and Noah stopped by the clinic to check on Gullipurr in the interim. His wounds were improving already. Now that he was feeling better, however, his willingness to be around people waned. It was as if his need for help had temporarily suppressed his feral tendencies. But Noah was winning him over with delectable wet food and plenty of treats. Gullipurr even took a treat from Lou's hand toward the end of their visit. It all felt like progress.

"We'll just need to stop by on our way back from the play tonight to give him his next dose of antibiotics," Noah said as they locked up and headed for the play.

All three couples arrived at Silver Lake High School within ten minutes of each other. Entering through the hall with the pictures, Lou pointed out the three teachers, so everyone was aware of what they looked like and could recognize them if they were, in fact, present for tonight's show.

"Okay, if anyone finds the bag, text the group so we can call off the other searches," Lou said, receiving nods and confirmation from the rest of the group. Splitting up, they headed inside.

Lou and Noah followed the signs for the stage, though they could've just as easily followed the stream of students rushing toward the large double doors at the end of the main hallway. In renaissance costumes, it wasn't hard to guess that they were each part of the production.

"If anyone asks, we're here to see our kid," Noah repeated their plan.

Lou tried not to obsess over the knowledge that the two of them could *technically* have a kid in high school. This week was not great when it came to her feeling young.

They followed a door that was marked Backstage and immediately dove into a rush of bodies. Students were everywhere. To their relief, there were also a few parent volunteers, so they didn't stick out as much.

Walking with intent, Lou pretended to know where she was going, striding through the throng of students preparing for their last performance. Makeup was being applied, hair was being coiffed, tears were being shed—Lou guessed those were from the seniors graduating next week —and lines were being practiced. But on the far side of it all, Lou spotted a small room in the back corner. A nameplate by the door marked it as an office.

Lou walked past it at first, continuing down the L-shaped hallway to see what else there was down that way, but mostly to find another exit if they needed it. When they passed by, there wasn't anyone inside the small room, so Lou doubled back and slipped inside, Noah following behind. He didn't shut the door, but he closed it enough that they weren't visible from the backstage area.

Right away, it became clear that they wouldn't need to stay there long. Boxes had been piled inside, each marked with a different play the high schoolers had performed over the years. Miss Klegg clearly wasn't using this space as her office, which meant they needed to find her classroom. Slinking back into the hallway, they continued their search, getting lucky when a girl arrived late and everyone barked at her to put her stuff in Miss Klegg's room *fast* so she could get her hair and makeup done.

They followed the girl, at a distance, watching as she rushed into a classroom just down the hall from one of the main backstage entrances. Waiting until she'd jogged back toward the stage, they entered the classroom in her place.

The room was warm and huge, piled with things just like the office had been. Instead of boxes, however, the classroom was full of student backpacks, water bottles, and other personal effects they were leaving back here during the show. Rather than containing regular desks, as one might expect in a formal classroom, the drama classroom had a tiered floor design that made the space into a small amphitheater of sorts.

While Lou was entranced by the room, Noah zeroed in on Miss Klegg's desk. Snapping his fingers, he motioned to a tote bag sitting next to her office chair. It was the very same bag Lou had seen in her bookshop that day—the one they'd both seen on the security footage. Pins littered the surface. An empty spot near the bottom corner held a pinhole, the place where the honor society pin had been.

Miss Klegg had to be the same woman who'd checked the note that day.

Excitement welled inside Lou, and she froze, unsure what to do next. *Text the group,* Lou's mind answered for her. Right. She pulled out her phone and sent the text.

> The drama teacher's our lady. The rest of you can stop searching.

George responded first.

> Great, because this Miss Heller has everything locked up and we're peering through her tiny windows like creeps.

A text came through from Easton next.

> Mrs. Cowell didn't lock anything, but she's so messy that I doubt we would've been able to find a thing. Heading back to the stage.

That taken care of, Lou turned to Noah, who was taking a picture of the bag. "Should we ... go too?" she asked.

"This should be enough for Easton to bring her in for questioning, right?"

"The faster we can get out of here, the better."

As much as Lou agreed, she couldn't help but let her gaze linger on the large calendar hanging behind Miss Klegg's desk. School functions, as well as the performances of *As You Like It*, were penciled in. But in red, there were other weekly additions having to do with a writing group, it seemed. Her high school customer had mentioned that Miss Klegg was a writer.

Submit chapters for critique was on the first of the month. Then, on the subsequent weeks, she'd written herself reminders to *Finish reading* Starlight Kingdom *chapters and email to S and T, Get notes to R about book 2,* and *Read and critique revised beginning of* A Journey Into the Soul. A big red *Critique Group* was written in on the last Saturday of the month.

Lou's gaze locked on the title of the last work in progress Miss Klegg was supposed to critique. It itched at the back of her mind.

"What is it?" Noah asked, his hand settling on her lower back as he noticed her attention on the calendar.

"I know this book," she whispered. But even as she said it, she couldn't be sure from where.

Footsteps stomped in their direction. It sounded like a whole herd of people was heading their way.

Noah and Lou locked eyes. Before they could move, the door swung open, and a group of four teenage girls spilled into the space. Their excited chatter stopped as they noticed the adults in the room.

"Sorry," Lou said. "We got lost. Could you tell us where the auditorium is?"

The girls mumbled something about it being down the hall to the left, suddenly shy when they'd been bubbly and outgoing only seconds before.

Thanking them, Lou grabbed Noah's hand and pulled him after her out of the classroom and toward their friends.

CHAPTER 20

T he other two couples were already seated by the time Lou and Noah made their way into the auditorium. Because they were so early, they got great seats, right in the center. George sat with a rigid discomfort as Lou took the seat beside her.

"What?" Lou asked, sensing there was something she wasn't saying.

Wesley glanced around, making sure there was no one within earshot before saying, "Just before you got here, we realized that we saw these renaissance-type costumes on the security footage for the burglary Thursday night at the candy store."

Lou cringed at the reminder. She hadn't seen any of that footage. Then her mind made a jump from the nun costumes they'd seen on the burglars during the florist job to something Silas had said weeks earlier. "Which means Silas was right about the guy he saw in lederhosen in my shop," she scoffed.

Only George had been there for that conversation, and

she filled in the others so they knew what Lou was talking about.

"Knowing Silas, he could've been describing one of these people in pantaloons." Lou gestured to one of the actors rushing across the stage as they set up.

"Or the lederhosen could've been from *The Sound of Music* too," George added.

Lou touched her nose. "Either way, I'm pretty sure that guy in costume is responsible for the first Gulliver book finding its way back into my shop."

"Well, that answers the question about how involved this drama teacher is in the whole scheme," Noah said. "She's not a pawn just picking up or dropping off locations if she's been supplying them with costumes."

"Did you get a picture of the tote?" Easton whispered, leaning forward since he was on the opposite end of their group.

Noah tapped his phone. "I have it."

"Should we stay?" Willow asked, wrinkling her nose.

Everyone tensed, all of them equally torn.

"I definitely don't have enough for an arrest warrant," Easton said, checking around them again, but they remained the only people in that section. "And I'm not going to pull her for questioning before their final performance. I'll wait until after, when most of the kids have gone home, to bring her into the station. The rest of you don't have to stay if you're uncomfortable."

Wesley snorted. "Is it weird that I kinda want to see this play? I've been really into romantic stories lately." He smirked at George, who jabbed her elbow into him playfully.

"Not weird at all. This is one of my favorite Shakespeare plays." A corner of Lou's mouth lifted. "It's all about becoming good friends first, before you fall in love." She threaded her fingers through Noah's.

Noah leaned over and kissed her. "Then I'm all in."

Willow took Easton's hand too. "We'll stay with you."

The detective's large shoulders settled, and if Lou wasn't mistaken, he looked relieved to have them as backup.

The theater filled in, and they weren't able to speak discreetly any longer, so they moved on to asking how George and Wesley's date had gone.

"Obviously, you made it through this one," Willow said, jerking her chin to Wesley and George's closeness.

The young couple grinned. "We did," they said at the same time.

A few students came onto the stage then and started a little comedy sketch while the audience found their seats, so they turned their attention forward. Lou hated to admit it, since their teacher was involved with a nefarious group of thieves and murderers, but she was obviously a very good drama teacher. Just as the high school student who'd come into her shop the other day had reported, each of the students had a hunger, a spark, a love for drama that shone through in everything they did.

Despite the great acting and the story being one of Lou's favorites, she couldn't fully enjoy herself during the performance. Worries about how their confrontation afterward would go overshadowed everything else, and she found herself zoning out during entire scenes.

When the play finally ended, Lou's torture wasn't over.

They still had to wait for the rest of the audience and most of the students to leave. Easton was adamant that pulling their teacher in for questioning in front of her students would not win him her cooperation. It was better to be discreet, especially until they were sure of the depth of her involvement.

"First to arrive. Last to leave." George whistled as she realized they were, in fact, the only people left in the seats.

They got up and wandered back to the classroom Lou and Noah had found earlier. They'd waited long enough. Only one student remained, it seemed, and he called a goodbye over his shoulder as he let the door swing shut behind him. A doorstop prevented it from closing all the way and light spilled out from the crack, proving the drama teacher was still there.

Easton knocked on the door.

Miss Klegg called out an absent-minded, "Did you forget something, Orion?"

Easton waited a moment and then knocked again. "Miss Klegg?"

The wheels of an office chair squeaked, and then the door flew open. Her gaze moved from Easton to the rest of them in surprise. "Oh, I'm so sorry. I thought you were my last student saying goodbye. Can I help you with something?"

There was a light behind her eyes as she asked, as if she was fairly sure they'd come to tell her how wonderfully the students had done, and how much they'd enjoyed the play. But then her gaze settled on Lou, and understanding swept through her.

"Denise Klegg?" Easton asked. When she nodded, he

said, "I'm Detective West from the Button Police Department." He showed his badge. "I need to ask that you come with me to the Button police station. I have some questions for you surrounding recent thefts in the county."

Her face blanched. "I, uh—" She gulped. "I can't." There was a quaver to her voice.

"Can't?" Easton straightened his spine, as if preparing for a confrontation.

"Can we talk here?" she asked quickly, her fingers clasping together in front of her. "I'll tell you whatever you want here, but I can't go to the police station. If I do, he'll see." She looked around them, as if someone else might've followed them down the hallway.

Clearing his throat, Easton frowned. "Who will see?"

Denise Klegg hitched a thumb to the classroom behind her. "Come in. We can talk in my classroom. It's a little more private."

The group filed into the room when she opened the door and stepped aside. Lou and her friends perched on the first tier of the amphitheater seating, but Easton remained standing, blocking the door just in case the woman tried to bolt.

"Okay, who are you worried will see?" he repeated his earlier question once the door shut behind him—all the way now that the doorstop had been kicked aside.

Miss Klegg worried her hands. "About a month ago, I was here late. It was a Friday night, and I was finishing up some props for the play since a few of my students came down with the flu and got behind on their sets. It was dark, so when I went into the parking lot, I didn't notice that there was a man hiding in the shadows next to the building." She swallowed, catching her breath. "He came out, holding me at gunpoint, and told me that he needed my help. He said if I didn't help him, he would hurt my dad. He even knew the nursing home he's staying in right now. He told me exactly how he'd get by security and how he'd convince him to come with him. My dad has dementia. He's all I've got, and I'm all he has." A tear streamed down the woman's cheek. "So, I told him I would do whatever he asked. He said to watch for instructions and left before I could ask what instructions I should watch for."

The group leaned forward. Easton's leg tensed as if he wanted to take a step toward her, but he leaned back into the door instead.

"The first note showed up on my windshield a few days later. It told me to keep my car unlocked while I was parked at school and that something would be deposited into the trunk. The next day, there was a book." She wrinkled her nose. "I think it was *Gulliver's Travels*? The note attached said I was supposed to put it in a certain section of the bookstore in Button with all the cats." At that, her attention flicked to Lou, her brow furrowing in a silent apology. "And things went on like that. Sometimes I needed to drop off a book. Other times I was supposed to pick up the note slipped inside the book. A few times it was requests like, leave three costumes in your trunk tomorrow, or another time it was four costumes." She shrugged.

"And you never thought to tell the police?" Easton asked with a sigh.

Denise Klegg's bottom lip stuck out. "Well, I figured he would watch me to make sure I didn't, that he would hurt my dad if I did. Plus, other than the scary way he approached me, none of it seemed all that bad. I was just sending notes and setting out costumes. He even returned the costumes in my trunk a few days later."

Lou's mind whirred with the revelation. So, Miss Klegg might've actually been a pawn, after all, nothing more than a messenger, unaware of who—and what—she was aiding.

"Well, those notes were helping thieves rob and burglarize local businesses, Miss Klegg," Easton said, his tone sharp and cutting. "And those harmless thieves killed a woman in our town when they broke in to rob her clothing boutique."

The only sound that Denise made was a small, "Oh."

Pacing now, Easton asked, "This man who approached you in the parking lot, can you remember anything about him?"

Miss Klegg screwed up her face and looked at the ceiling. "I, uh—well, it was really dark. He was very tall. I remember that."

Lou's heart caught in her throat. Tall. Like the person who'd shot Heather.

The teacher kept rambling nervously. "Though his height could've been because he was wearing cowboy boots and they had chunky heels. But other than that, his face was covered, and I didn't recognize his voice."

Tall with cowboy boots. Lou had heard that before. Her heartbeat quickened.

Easton ran a hand down his face. "Okay." He pulled out a card from his wallet. "This is my personal number. If you get any other notes from this man, I need you to contact me. Is that clear?"

The drama teacher took the card with a reverence usually reserved for fine porcelain. "I will. I promise."

"And I might call on you for more questions." Easton fixed her with a serious stare.

She nodded back, matching his expression.

Jerking his head toward the door, Easton said, "Let's go."

The five of them followed his lead, filing out of the classroom. It wasn't until they'd passed through a few doors and were in the hallway alone that Easton stopped.

"Debrief at our house?" he asked, greeting a custodian who walked down the hall. It was a different one than the other day when Lou and Noah had been there. Likely the night custodian.

Everyone agreed and headed for the parking lot. All except Lou. She stood frozen by the display case in the entryway, the one with pictures of the staff members.

"Lou?" Noah asked, placing a hand on her arm.

She could sense the rest of her friends stopping too.

"Something she said back there, about the cowboy boots, it reminded me…" She trailed off as her eyes pored over the text written underneath each picture, giving the person's name and position. Finally, she found what she was looking for. "Him." She jabbed her finger at the glass.

Soles of shoes squeaked on the linoleum floor as her friends crowded around her to see who she was pointing at.

"Rich Neville? Campus security?" George read aloud.

But Lou couldn't answer, because while she'd heard that very phrase about the security guard being tall, but possibly only because he wore cowboy boots, from the high school boy in her shop, she'd also seen his picture before too.

"He's the author who wrote the horror book I found on my shelf." Lou pulled the paperback out of her purse. She turned to George. "The one you found."

"R. G. Stillhouse is the pen name for Rich Neville," Willow said, her words breathy.

Lou bobbed her head slowly. "And I think he's connected to, if not running, these thefts."

Easton snapped a photograph of Rich's picture. "Can I borrow that?" he asked, holding out a hand for the book.

"You can keep it." Lou shivered, glad the offending novel was finally out of her possession.

"Okay, *now* we should reconvene at our place," Easton said, frowning at his phone. "I've got a few phone calls to make on the way, but hopefully I'll have some news by the time we're back in Button."

They split up in the parking lot. Lou rehashed, in more detail now that they knew it was important to the case, all the disturbing things she'd read in Rich's book as Noah drove, and by the time they arrived home, the shivery feeling sitting on her spine had become a full tingle.

"Oh, can you let me out here? I'll grab the mail." Lou opened the passenger door once Noah stopped.

She slipped out, grabbing the mail before walking back to the car. Noah had pulled off onto the shoulder a few yards ahead. She passed by their Little Free Library, but instead of her usual quick glance as she walked by, Lou stopped dead in her tracks.

With shaking fingers, Lou tucked the mail under her left

arm and opened the small door to the Little Free Library. Inside was a hardback. A specially illustrated edition of *Gulliver's Travels.*

CHAPTER 21

These thieves—the ones who'd killed Heather, the very people who'd been terrorizing local businesses—knew where she lived. That terrifying reality made her feel like an unwary beachgoer swamped by a sneaker wave. She tottered unsteadily back to where Noah had the car idling and sank back into the passenger seat, the book thunking into her lap.

His gaze darkened. "I see closing didn't help as much as we'd hoped."

But Lou couldn't answer. She'd opened the book and discovered a piece of paper slipped inside. Just as with the others she'd found, it held a typed paragraph. Random letters were positioned lower than others, signifying the code that would tell them when and where the next burglary or robbery would take place.

Despite all the similarities, this excerpt was different. This one, she remembered. Vividly.

"We need to get inside," Lou whispered as her eyes snagged on the choppy text.

In front of him stood a walrus of a man. In fact, he looked so very unhealthy that he might drop dead from a heart attack at any second. A layer of sweat gathered on his neck, upper lip, and brow. A shiver of disgust moved up his back. "Sick."

Describing characters in unflattering ways wasn't uncommon in the literary world. Comparing a person to something like a walrus or an elephant wasn't something she saw a lot toward the end of her career as an editor. Even the confusing overuse of male pronouns when there were two separate male characters in the same scene could be fixed in editing. But the really disturbing line had been the one about the heart attack.

Lou had read that very line two years prior, just after losing Ben to a heart attack. Hearing the cause of her husband's death used in such a cavalier, judgmental way had felt like a gut punch.

George and Wesley pulled into the shared driveway, followed by Easton and Willow. Noah drove up behind them, and they all piled inside Willow and Easton's house.

"Did you talk to the Silver Lake police?" Wesley asked as they entered.

"I did. They're a little nervous about getting a warrant on the evidence we've got, so they're going to see if they can't catch him in the act at one of the burglaries. Oh, Lou, is that another book?" His focus was locked on Lou and what she held in her hands. "Where'd you get that?"

"She just found it in our Little Free Library," Noah explained, seeing Lou was still stuck in her thoughts.

Blinking, she tried to snap out of it. They needed to know what she'd just realized.

"I know where these passages have been coming from," Lou said, walking past everyone to place the most recent note on the dining room table. "I've had a feeling all along that they're familiar, but I couldn't place them until now, until this." She gestured to the paper.

Craning their necks, her friends read it over.

"The passages aren't from Rich's horror novel. They're from a manuscript I rejected during my last few weeks as an editor back in New York City," Lou explained.

It hadn't been the worst writing she'd ever read, by far, but it had rubbed her the wrong way from the start. It could've been the main character's innate misogyny or the author's tendency toward prose so purple it made Lou's brain hurt that had made her want to pass on the manuscript. Those things had certainly edged her toward a rejection, but when she'd read *that* line, the one about a heart attack, it had solidified her decision.

"That's why it sounded familiar, but it isn't published." Frowning, she added, "And Denise must be in a critique group with the guy who wrote it." Remembering the writing on the calendar, she amended, "Who's *still* writing it. *A Journey Into the Soul.*"

"Wait." Willow shook her head, a long blink working to erase her confusion. "Are we talking about the same guy who wrote the horror novel?"

"I don't think so," Lou said. "The writing's too different. They have to be two separate authors. But I think Denise might be in a critique group with both of them. On her calendar, she had reminders to herself to send her chapters in for submission to her critique partners. But she also had deadlines for getting them feedback on their stuff. In addition to reading the new beginning to *A Journey Into the Soul,* one of Denise's reminders to herself said *send notes to R about book* 2. I believe 'R' is short for Rich and—"

"He's writing a second one of those?" George cried out in alarm, interrupting Lou.

Easton closed his eyes. "Which means we're dealing with two authors from her group, not just one. And it also means that she would have recognized Rich if he was the one who approached her in the parking lot." He exhaled in frustration as he realized Denise had lied to him.

Lou cringed. "Yeah, I have a bad feeling everything we saw in there was an act. Unfortunately, she's not just a good teacher, she's also a good actor. I think Denise and her critique group are the ones behind the thefts."

Noah snapped his fingers. "And Rich is probably the tall person who shot Heather."

"If he's in security, even school security, I'd bet he knows how to handle a gun." Willow pursed her lips.

"But some jobs had three and four people," George argued, having been the one looking at the surveillance footage of the break-ins the most.

"And neither Rich nor Denise dropped off that kitten on the first day?" Wesley asked.

"No," Lou said, sure about that, at least. "I don't remember much about them, but they were definitely closer to your and George's age than mine."

Easton grabbed his keys. "I'm going to Silver Lake. I've got to pay their station a visit."

"Wait," Lou called. She pointed to the note on the table. "Let's figure out where they're going to hit next. It could be tonight, and they might be able to catch them in the act."

Expression softening, as if he couldn't believe he'd forgotten that, Easton walked back over as Lou rewrote the designated letters below. "The third day would be Sunday, tomorrow, but they've broken patterns before just to mess with us, so I wouldn't put it past them to hit tonight." He stopped to check over Lou's shoulder as she circled the letters.

Just as with the last one, there wasn't a time listed, but the location made everyone freeze.

In front of him stood a walrus of a man. In fact, he looked so very unhealthy that he might drop dead from a heart attack at any second. A layer of sweat gathered on his neck, upper lip, and brow. A shiver of disgust moved up his back. "Sick."

silver lake books

"Silver Lake Books," George said aloud.

"Okay, so it looks like I'm going to have to make a stop *before* I go visit the Silver Lake station," Easton amended.

"We can warn Austin," Wesley offered, stepping forward next to George. "You worry about getting the police ready, and we'll let Austin know he's next on the list. He's got a ton of security cameras around the place, so if you guys don't catch them in the act, I'm sure it'll be enough to get a warrant."

"Thank you." Easton tossed his keys in the air and caught them. "I'll be in touch."

With that, George and Wesley left in their car to warn Austin, and Easton went to gather the support of his fellow officers. Once it was just Lou, Noah, and Willow, they sighed and traded resigned glances.

"I guess we'll just stay here," Willow said, a little crestfallen.

Lou chuckled, finding it hard to keep her emotions in check after the roller coaster of an evening.

"This *Journey Into the Soul* book you hated..." Noah scratched at his cheek. "You don't remember the author?"

"I don't. But..." She realized with a jolt that she knew who would. Lou pulled out her phone. "Hold on." Her fingers flew over her phone screen as she opened her email app and typed in the address of her former editorial assistant, Amber.

"I may not remember his name, but I remember the situation surrounding his manuscript being brought to my attention, and I know Amber will too." She typed out an urgent email subject line, asking Amber to get back to her as soon as possible. After a concise question, Lou sent the email, then turned to Willow and Noah to explain herself. "Amber was an editorial assistant right before I stepped down. She came in one day with a manuscript she wouldn't stop raving about. She said she'd found it in the pile of unrepresented submissions—authors who send in their books without an agent. I don't think that manuscript would've been for me in any circumstance, but it really rubbed me the wrong way when the main character described the man as looking as if he was going to have a heart attack. It was weeks after I'd lost Ben, and it felt like I was transported back to that day, crying in the park. I told Amber I was going to pass on it and asked her to write up our standard rejection letter. But Amber freaked out, saying she'd already promised him it would be a hit, and how could she go back on that now?"

Willow and Noah exchanged a wary glance.

"Apparently, the author was a handsome guy she'd seen working at a local coffee shop near her apartment. She'd been watching him for a while and was trying to get up the courage to talk to him, when she realized the thing he was always working on was a novel. She approached him, bragging that she was an assistant at a publishing house and that she could get his manuscript in front of an editor."

The two grimaced at Amber's faux pas.

Lou clicked her tongue as if scolding the Amber in the story as well. "She'd been so dazzled by his attention that she'd made promises she shouldn't have, promises she couldn't deliver on, especially when I didn't like it."

"What happened?" Willow asked.

Noah leaned closer. "Did Amber get fired?"

"No," Lou said. "I convinced my bosses not to, that I believed it was a momentary lapse in judgment. She was so grateful to keep her job, and I even wrote a specific rejection letter, clarifying that it was my issue with the novel, not anything Amber had done wrong."

Noah's features softened. "That was sweet of you."

Lou shrugged. "We'll see if she—"

But she didn't get to finish that thought because her phone began buzzing with an incoming call. Worried it might be George or Easton, Lou glanced at the screen.

Amber was calling her.

"It's gotta be midnight on the East Coast," Lou mumbled before answering the call. "Hello?" Lou asked, wary.

"Lou?" Amber's voice was entirely too loud at the best of times, but it sounded like she was shouting over the sounds of a party in the background.

"Amber, hey. What's up? Did you get my email?" Lou didn't mean for the question to sound rude, but it held an air of *Could this have been an email instead of a call?*

"I did!" she said excitedly. "I just figured it would be easier to call you."

Suddenly, the memories from the months she'd worked with Amber came back to hit her in the face. The fast talking, the volume with which she said everything, and the way she refused to answer questions over email, instead preferring to "talk it out." The young woman was definitely the exception to her generation in that respect.

"No problem. You've got me. So, do you remember that guy? *A Journey Into the Soul?*"

She snorted. "Of course I do. I thought for sure the two of us were soul mates for the better part of a year."

Lou wasn't going to apologize for doing her job, and she'd bailed Amber out of the situation she'd created as best she could.

"But it's okay. It was probably for the best," Amber said, almost as if Lou had apologized.

"Why?"

"He got pretty aggressive when I gave him the rejection letter and told him you didn't like his book."

Lou couldn't see Amber, but she could picture the bouncy young woman pulling a face as she said that last sentence.

"And do you remember his name?" Lou asked. "I could only remember the name of the manuscript."

"Yeah," Amber scoffed. "It was J. A. Cook."

Lou frowned. That was a common last name. "Cook?"

"Mmm hmm. But he went by his middle name," Amber explained. "Which, for some reason, made me absolutely certain he and I were meant to be." She giggled at herself. "Obviously, that was before I met Winston," she said dreamily. "Have I told you about Winston yet? Oh, or how he proposed?"

She was definitely jumping up and down. It was the same thing she did anytime she found an amazing manuscript she thought Lou would love, which was often. Despite this one instance, Amber had been very good at her job.

"You haven't." Lou kept her voice measured. "And I'd love to hear all about him, but I really need to know everything you can remember about J. A. Cook, Amber. It's kind of a life-or-death scenario over here."

"Austin," Amber said.

Lou blinked. "What?"

"His middle name. That's what he went by. Austin. Jonathan Austin Cook, but he wrote under J. A. Cook and told me his friends all called him Austin."

Austin Cook. The new owner of Silver Lake Books. The very man who'd been heading up the combined efforts of the local chambers of commerce in an effort to stop the thefts.

Lou's whole body went hot, then cold. "Austin," she said in a choked voice, meeting Willow's and Noah's gazes. They both paled with fear.

"Gosh, I haven't thought about him in years. I wonder if he ever found someone to publish that book of his?" Amber mused, unaware of the apoplectic state Lou was in.

"I can guarantee you, he didn't," Lou said, her voice strained and scratchy.

Amber let out a sharp laugh. "Yeah, I guess it was pretty bad writing. I'll admit that I got caught up in how he looked. He was also really nice too. Attentive and thought-ful," she added, as if Lou might judge her for only being interested in Austin for shallow reasons.

"I'm so sorry, Amber, but I really have to go," Lou said quickly, hanging up before Amber launched into another long-winded story.

Her heart clenched with worry.

"George and Wesley are heading straight for him," Noah said, grabbing his phone. "We have to warn them."

CHAPTER 22

Willow's phone was in her hand as well. "You warn George. I'll call Easton." She stepped into the other room.

Lou moved closer to Noah, trying to hear his conversation.

Noah's dark brows contracted, creating a deep divot on his forehead. Finally, his face softened. "George, I need you to stop what you're doing and listen."

Lou heard a nervous giggle come through the phone. "Uh, okay?" George said, but it was wrapped in a question.

"Austin Cook is also part of Denise's writing group. He's been behind this all along. If you are with him now, you need to leave." Noah's voice was firm, measured.

"Austin?" George gasped. "Wesley, Austin's the one who wrote the book Lou rejected."

Noah glanced at Lou, his eyes narrowing momentarily. She knew he was frustrated by their lack of communication.

"We're not with him," George said. "He's not at his

house and isn't answering his phone, so we left a message. We went to Wesley's."

"Stay there," Noah warned. "Don't leave, and don't take any calls from Austin if he returns your message, okay? Easton and the Silver Lake police know his bookshop is a target, so even if we're wrong, they'll check into it."

"Got it," George said, finally understanding the fear that had gripped them in the moment.

Willow returned, phone by her side as Noah ended his call with George.

"They're safe. Austin wasn't around," Noah told Willow, knowing Lou had overheard that part.

The three of them sank onto Willow's sofa, exhaling out simultaneous sighs of relief.

"What a stressful night." Lou's eyes fluttered closed as she snuggled deeper into the couch. "I feel so silly that I didn't see that it was Austin until now," she said around a yawn. "Noah, remember at dinner how he told us he'd inherited his grandfather's writing *paraphernalia*?" She emphasized the last word.

Noah snorted out a laugh. "Yeah, I'd bet anything it included an old typewriter."

"He told you that? It's like the guy was *trying* to get caught," Willow said. "He may as well pull a Gullipurr and jump right into a jail cell like Gullipurr jumped into that crate with you and Wesley. I mean, not that Gullipurr's in jail or any—"

Noah sat bolt upright. "Gullipurr," he said, looking at Lou. "I need to give him his next dose of the antibiotic."

"We forgot on our way back from the play," Lou groaned.

Noah patted her leg. "I'll go take care of him. I'll be right back."

"Thank you. I love you." Lou gazed up adoringly at him as he grabbed his keys and got ready to leave. Lou leaned her head against Willow's, and they sighed.

"I think I could sleep for a week," Willow said through a yawn.

Lou agreed, and she might've actually dozed off a little because the next thing she knew, she jerked awake as her phone beeped with a notification. It was the bookshop. The cats might've triggered the alarm, but Lou could've sworn she'd put them upstairs. Willow's breathing was measured and heavy next to Lou, so she opened the app quietly, turning down the volume.

There, in the middle of her shop, stood Austin Cook with a man she recognized from his picture on his author website. Rich Neville, the tall security guard, made even taller by the cowboy boots he wore. The very man who'd left that terrifying book on a shelf in her bookshop without her permission, and the person who'd shot Heather.

"Lou," Austin sang out, looking straight at the camera. "Come talk to me. I have a proposition for you."

She froze.

As if he could sense her indecision, Austin picked up Anne Mice and added, "It would be a shame if something happened to your cats. Oh, and don't think about calling the cops. If I hear a siren, I'll let Rich do his worst."

Anger boiled in Lou's chest. She'd read snippets of that man's horror novel. She knew he had a twisted soul.

Willow shifted, blinking her eyes open. "What did he just say?"

Vaulting up off the couch, Lou said, "I have to get there. He's going to hurt the cats."

"Whoa," Willow said, her hands patting the air. It was the exact thing she did when OC was riled up. "We shouldn't rush in there. Let's call the station and see if they can send a patrol car there while we wait for Ea—"

"Lou's not coming anywhere near you," Noah's voice rang through the speaker.

Lou's heart stopped. She held the phone up to her face as Noah stepped into the left of the frame. He must've slipped in through the back entrance. He looked directly at the camera, knowing she would be watching. She'd been the one to forget that there were two of them getting the notifications now.

"Listen carefully. You're going to put the cat down and step away. If you hurt any of them, you'll have to deal with me," Noah ground out, his tone deeper, fiercer than Lou had ever heard.

"Luckily, we brought something that'll help that conversation," Rich said, pointing a gun at Noah.

Willow and Lou looked at one another and ran for the door. Lou drove, and Willow called Easton on the way.

"I'll send everyone we've got there," Easton said, adding, "You and Lou stay in the car."

But Lou was already slamming the brakes, coming to a stop in the alley behind her bookstore. She'd heard Easton but couldn't leave Noah in there alone with a man who'd already shot and killed one person. With an apologetic glance, she threw open her door and started for the bookshop.

"Well, Lou just got out of the car," Willow whispered into the phone. "So, I don't think that's going to happen. Please be quick and come through the back." She hung up the call and slunk behind Lou as she came up to the bookshop.

Thanking Noah for leaving it unlocked—and for greasing the hinges so the door no longer squeaked, plus installing padding along the doorjamb so it didn't make a terrible banging noise—Lou slipped inside, followed by Willow. She hoped the police would get there quickly.

In the meantime, they needed to get Noah out of the way of the gun and the cats to safety. From that vantage point, she could see Noah's back to her. Austin and Rich faced that direction, but if she and Willow stayed low, they shouldn't be able to see them.

Creeping to her office, Lou eyed Willow once they were safe behind the door. They needed a distraction, something to hold Austin and Rich's attention long enough that they could at least knock that gun out of Rich's hand.

Lou thought through what she might be able to use as a distraction. They'd used a kitten and a plant on her. *Should I throw books at them? Hit them with their own tricks?* she wondered, glancing around her office. It was too bad she and Noah had slipped Prudence into Marigold's bag. That doll could've created the perfect, terrifying diversion. Alas, they were Prudence-less. But there was yet another of Marigold's possessions that had been corralled to the office. Lou's gaze settled on the pile of yarn on her desk.

"Thank you, Goldie," Lou whispered as she rushed over to gather the yarn into her arms.

Willow must've understood what she was going to do, because she held out her hands, ready to take some yarn as well.

"I suppose we can tell *you* our terms," Austin said, a nervous tinge to his voice. He must've known that the longer Lou didn't show up, the more likely it was that she'd called the police, but he'd yet to hurt Anne Mice. "We want her bookstore. And either she sells it to us for the price we set, or something will happen to each of her precious cats." He spoke more quickly, as if he knew he was running out of time.

"Really? This is their plan?" Willow whispered, scowling at the criminals. "It's not very good."

Lou agreed, but she was more concerned with how desperate they sounded, how willing they were to use fatal force when put in a corner. And at the moment, Noah and the cats were in that corner with them.

She needed to create a distraction, but Noah needed to be in on it. She wanted him out of the way if Rich was as trigger-happy as he appeared. Which meant that before she and Willow chucked a bunch of yarn into the shop, she needed to warn Noah that they were there.

Rolling one of the yarn balls carefully, Lou held on to the string, pulling back on it to slow its progress. She only wanted it to go as far as the first shelf, and she hoped Noah would see the movement out of the corner of his eye.

Of course, when she yanked on the yarn, the ball simply sped faster. But Noah stepped back at just the right moment, and the ball bounced off his shoe, heading back in the direction of the office before Austin or Rich could see it.

Lou panted in relief. By his side, Noah flexed his hand. At first, Lou thought he was recreating the Darcy hand movement she and Wesley had been discussing the other day, but she quickly realized he was counting down.

Four fingers. Three. Two. One.

"Now," Lou whispered.

She and Willow threw the yarn out into the bookshop, holding on to the ends so they streamed across the shop. Austin and Rich yelled out in confusion, and Noah took that opportunity to dive forward.

Lou's heart was in her throat as he dove out of her line of sight. No gunshot came.

Noah must've hit Rich right in the torso because the gun came flying forward, clattering to the floor.

"Rich," Austin scolded. "Get that gun. Ugh. Fine. I'll grab it." He tossed Anne Mice aside and rushed forward.

Lou did too. She couldn't let them get the weapon back. She felt Willow surge after her.

But all three of them stopped by the back door where the gun lay on the ground, a dark boot propped on top of it, pinning it to the floor.

Officer Reynolds stood there, a sly smile on his face, and his own firearm pointed at Austin. "Hands up, buddy," the cranky officer said.

Austin raised his arms over his head.

Lou had never wanted to hug the ornery officer, whose normal place was behind the reception desk, so much.

"Are you alone?" Willow asked, glancing over at Noah, who was still wrestling with Rich near the front of the store.

"Nope. Get in here, team. It's clear." Reynolds winked—

winked!—at Lou as officers from Silver Lake and Brine streamed through the back door.

They quickly cuffed Austin and Rich. Easton arrived minutes later, and he was about to take them in when Lou looked at Austin.

"So, this was about my bookstore this whole time, not your manuscript?" She needed to know.

Austin sneered in her direction. "Oh, it was always about the manuscript. You killed my dream. I remembered your name. I saved that terrible letter you wrote me. I reread it daily, every time I rewrote a chapter of my manuscript, every time I doubted myself." Spit flew out of his mouth as he surged toward her. All his suave charm was gone, and Lou wondered how she'd ever thought he was right for George.

Easton gripped his wrists tighter, clenching his jaw, but nodding at Lou that she was okay to continue.

"People like you killed all our dreams." He looked at Rich, but he must've also been talking about Denise and whoever else was in their group. "And even though you hadn't been the specific editor to write them their rejection letters, when I told them I'd found you in the next town over, and asked them if they wanted to help me ruin your life, they jumped at the chance. Getting back at one of you felt like we were getting back at everyone who'd ever told us no, to all the gatekeepers in their ivory towers."

Lou suppressed an eye roll.

"With my bookstore, and if we could get yours, too, we could simply publish our books and sell them ourselves." Austin's eyes were wild. "We would show you we didn't need you and your fancy publishing house."

"You never needed me." Lou shook her head as Noah came over to wrap an arm around her shoulder after making sure each of the cats was perfectly healthy. "If you had believed in yourself, you could've published it like Rich. The publishing world is changing." Lou had many books by self-published authors in the shop, especially local ones. "And what about George?" Lou asked.

Austin sneered. "A perfect distraction for the private investigator my fellow chamber of commerce members wanted to hire. I was already devising a plan to keep him looking in the wrong places, but when I saw the way he looked at George, I knew she was the perfect diversion."

"That's why you insisted that George remain the only one with password access? Why you forced them to work together?" Lou clicked her tongue in disappointment.

"And why I started dating her when I saw how much worse he got when he was jealous," Austin added. "You were all too easy to fool."

Still confused, Lou asked, "Why place the notes in my bookstore, though? You led us right to you."

Anger flashed over Austin's features. "It was supposed to mess with your head, to make you alienate your customers. If we made the locals question whether you were involved, that would just be a bonus. We were willing to try anything to push you toward closing your shop."

Easton must've decided that was enough, because he pushed Austin toward the door, unfazed by the thrashing and yelling Austin continued with as they walked. Leaning into Noah, Lou waited until the law enforcement officers were gone, and then she wrapped her arms around him, holding on tight.

Noah squeezed back, knowing she needed the pressure. Then, proving he always knew exactly what she needed, he said, "Who would've thought the heroes of the night would be Marigold's yarn and Officer Reynolds?"

Lou let her head fall back, and she laughed for the first time all night.

CHAPTER 23

"So, he really just refused to leave when you tried to let him go?" Gloria put a hand on her hip as if she couldn't believe her ears.

Lou chuckled, but confirmed the rumors were true. "Noah opened the crate, Gullipurr walked out, and then he strode back inside and wouldn't leave." She gazed fondly at the large orange cat.

She had yet to bring Sapphire and Lillipurrtian in—Lilli still had some growing to do, and the two were more than content at the house for now—but she couldn't wait for them to meet the newest foster to call Whiskers and Words home.

"He got used to the indoor cat life." Cricket grinned at the cat as he curled into a tight ball in one of the many fleece beds placed throughout the bookstore.

"He's still not super fond of people petting him, so we'll have to work on that," Lou said, noting that the cat kept each of them in his sight. "But I think Gullipurr's travels are officially done."

"Ready to become a recluse and spend hours a day talking to his horses in the stables," Silas muttered, proving he'd read his copy of *Gulliver's Travels* since Lou had talked to him last.

Everyone laughed.

"Let's hope not," George snorted.

The bell on the door rang, and Wesley strode inside. Strapped to his chest was Geralt, snug and happy in the baby wrap George usually wore him in. Lou suppressed a grin, glancing briefly at Forrest and sharing a small smile.

"Wesley, fatherhood looks good on you, doll." Cricket flashed a big smirk at the young man. Her grin only widened when she shifted her attention to George.

Lou had to admit that her friend seemed incredibly happy.

Wesley puffed out his chest. "Thanks, Crick. Gerry and I are getting along pretty well."

George's lips tugged downward. "Wesley," she snapped. "I told you not to call him Gerry. That's *not* his name."

Wesley snagged George around the waist and pulled her close. She stiffened, pretending she didn't want to embrace Wesley back, but once she was close enough, Geralt leaned forward and licked the tip of her nose. George's serious expression broke, and she cradled her cat's head in her hands.

Marigold came strolling into the room, a small herd of foster cats trailing her and the scarf she was knitting—well, more like the many strings flying off the scarf she was knitting. She plopped onto the couch next to Silas, nodded matter-of-factly at the older man, and then began knitting while he read his newspaper.

Marigold was officially out of school for the summer, and Lou was more than happy to have her at the bookshop with her when she could. The girl was signed up for a few camps, and spent time with both her sets of grandparents, but Lou took her the rest of the time. She'd even started accompanying Lou on some of her runs.

"You made the paper," Silas grumbled, loudly cracking the page back as he showed Lou the article that had been written up about Austin and his writing group, and how they'd been behind the burglaries and robberies happening in the area.

Lou had read the copy already. She'd requested to have her name left out, merely showing up as "local business owners helped police track down the suspects."

"So, the tall one is the only one charged with murder?" Gloria asked, hand on her hip again.

Cricket snorted out a laugh. "After he tried to plead that he was merely defending himself because she pointed the gun at him, and he's trained in self-defense gun maneuvers, so he couldn't help that his training kicked in."

They all rolled their eyes.

Forrest tilted his head. "The others are being charged as accessories. They won't get off scot-free, even with all the backstabbing and tattling they did."

He wasn't wrong. The writers' group had apparently been crumbling under a toxic environment already. Denise didn't really want to read any more of Rich's horror novels. Sully and Tosh, the two younger men Lou had met when they'd brought Lilli in that first day—and the same two who'd staged the plant distraction—were cowriting an epic fantasy together, and "broke up" their writing partnership about once a week, only to be back at it the next day. And no one wanted to read any more versions of Austin's novel. Denise complained that she'd already read twenty different opening chapters, and that the man needed to just pick one already.

But when Rich killed Heather, the group agreed on one thing: their plan had officially gone too far. Rich, however, lived up to his creepy novel and blackmailed them into continuing, saying it was too late to go back now.

Given the cracks that were already present, they'd folded on each other almost immediately.

"Good riddance," Silas huffed.

Wesley's eyebrows curved up. "With Austin out of the picture, I hear Silver Lake Books is going up for sale. Lou, are you sure you don't want a second location of Whiskers and Words?"

She cut the air with her hand. "I've got my hands full with this one. I'm completely content."

WHISKERS AND WORDS WILL RETURN ...

Scratched Off, book 11, will be coming in 2025!

Join Eryn Scott's mailing list to learn about new releases and sales!

Whiskers and Words Mysteries

Ongoing series * Best friends *
Bookshop full of cats

PEPPER BROOKS
COZY MYSTERY SERIES

Completed series * Literary mysteries * Sweet romance * Cute dog

ABOUT THE AUTHOR

Eryn Scott lives in the Pacific Northwest with her husband and their quirky animals. She loves classic literature, musicals, knitting, and hiking. She writes cozy mysteries and women's fiction.

Join her mailing list to learn about new releases and sales!

www.erynscott.com

9 798348 514587